DOPPELGÄNGER

DOPPELGÄNGER

by Susan Cory

Dedicated to Zack and Alice

PROLOGUE

"No way." Rosica Bakalov stared more closely at the picture on the monitor. It was like looking in a mirror—the same slightly curved nose and pale skin. The same almond-shaped eyes, although Rosica's were green, not brown.

She liked to scroll through the photo files on the computers she was mining for IDs in case there were any interesting shots she could sell to porn sites. She'd been less than impressed with most of the soft-core stuff that these amateurs thought was racy.

But this discovery was a potential gold mine. A mark who could be her twin. Granted, the hair was different, but Rosica had dyed her hair so often she could barely remember her natural color. Plus, the woman was older by maybe a dozen years in the latest photos, but she was in good shape. What was her name? Rosica clicked back to the woman's financial file: Iris Reid.

IRIS

CHAPTER ONE

Iris Reid caught her breath as she gazed at the decrepit Victorian house on Massachusetts Avenue, Cambridge's main drag. The lead-gray March sky lent the property a bleak appearance. The peeling mauve paint made it seem almost ghostly.

"It's perfect," she said to her boyfriend, Luc Cormier.

"Doesn't look much like a restaurant." Luc stared skeptically at the sloping porch floor and rotted clapboards. "Looks like it should be condemned."

Iris slid out the listing sheet from her parka's pocket. "But look at the price. There'll be money left over to fix it up. And it's got ten parking spaces in back."

"You know how parking gets me excited," Luc conceded. His present restaurant, located three blocks away, had no off-street parking. That, along with his landlord's decision to double his rent was driving Luc to find a new location for the Paradise Café. Plus the need for more space to accommodate his devoted clientele.

Light snow began to fall. Iris' long brown hair was stuffed up into her hat and she felt a cold, wet snowdrop slither down the back of her neck.

"Let's go inside," she said, "and see if the interior holds as much potential as the exterior."

As Luc pushed open the creaking front door, Iris smelled mustiness in the air. She could hear the musical chatter of their broker, Bala Bhat, talking on her cell phone in the entryway. Bala gave them an excited wave, her bracelets jangling, and winding down her conversation, turned her attention to them. "This is the perfect property for you, Luc. And with Iris being an architect, you won't be put off by all the little tweaks it needs."

"Tweaks," Luc mumbled as he eyed the faded wallpaper in the entry hall and gloomy rooms to either side. "This may be more than we can manage. I need to have a restaurant up and running in seven months."

Iris did a 360. She took in the high ceilings, the large windows behind the dusty drapes, and the open flow of the two large rooms, one of which had an ornate fireplace. "Was this a single family house, Bala? The listing says it's around 5000 square feet."

"It was built as a grand old mansion. Now it's zoned for both commercial and residential." Bala pointed a vermilion-nailed finger straight up. "You could live above the shop if you wanted."

"Sell my condo and combine spaces?" Luc ran a hand through his shoulder-length blond hair. "That could make the numbers work."

"And if you didn't mind a tenant in the basement, you could get additional rent from the woman who teaches yoga classes down there at night," Bala said. "But the sale isn't contingent on keeping her. She has a month-to-month lease and pays $1000 per month."

"Might work, but I'd probably need that space for food storage." Luc wandered toward the back of the house.

Following him, Iris ran her fingers over the mahogany wainscoting lining the walls. Abruptly, a door swung open and its doorknob smacked her in the stomach before she could step out of the way.

"Oof," Iris said.

Luc grabbed and steadied her just as a young woman squeezed into the hallway beside them.

"Sorry. I didn't know anyone was up here." The woman fixed large hazel eyes on Iris, concerned. "Are you all right?"

Iris took in a gulp of air and wheezed out "Fine."

The woman, extremely slim and fit in her yoga pants and tight top, caught sight of Luc and smiled. "Are you two thinking of buying this place?"

"Considering it," Luc answered. "You rent space in the basement?"

"I have my yoga studio down there and a small office. I was just catching up on some paperwork. If you do buy the building, I'd love to continue renting. I'm Hannah." She reached out to shake Luc's hand, then Iris'.

"If we get to that point, we can give you a call," Iris answered. "Do you have a card?"

The woman tapped her clothes which clearly allowed no room for pockets. "Not with me, but I can write down my number. Have you got any paper and a pen?"

Bala, who'd been checking messages on her phone in the more spacious entry hall, bustled forward to offer both from her cavernous purse.

Scribbling for a moment, Hannah handed the paper to Luc. "That's my cell. You should come to my yoga class. It's a great stress reliever." She glanced over at Iris. "You, too."

Hannah slid behind Luc and placed her hands on his shoulders, thumbs on the blades. "Just as I thought," she announced. "Completely stiff. You work hunched over, right?"

Luc explained that he was a chef.

Hannah pulled Luc's shoulders back so he was standing straighter. "This is how you should stand when you're at the counter."

"Yeah, that does feel better." Luc turned to Iris. "Didn't I just say that my back's been bothering me lately?"

"Mmhmm." Iris noted Hannah's long firm legs and tight abs. She pegged the yogini at late twenties, too naturally pretty to bother wearing make-up. Iris was approaching her mid forties and Luc was six years her junior.

"Let's check out the kitchen," Iris reached for Luc's hand.

Hannah headed for the front door. "Even if you don't buy the building, you really need to come to my Bikram class, Luc. You know—hot yoga. It would do wonders to stretch out your muscles."

Luc turned to watch her leave. "Doesn't Hannah smell like cinnamon bread?"

"Wow—this kitchen hasn't been touched since the 1940's," Iris said, changing the subject. "It's a nice size. I'd have to make some changes with all these windows and doors to give you continuous counters."

"This is four times the size of what I'm cooking in now."

"...And we'd have to carve out some space for bathrooms and a coat room."

After they'd explored the room in detail, Luc leaned against one of the oversized windows, staring out at a yard blanketed in a foot of pristine snow. He shoved his hands deep in the pockets of his coat. "Are you sure we wouldn't be biting off too much? Assuming I could dig up the small fortune it would all cost, could this place even be ready by September?"

Iris joined him at the window. She could visualize a property completely transformed. She could sense the beauty that could be coaxed out of the present reality. "This is your new restaurant. Trust me."

CHAPTER TWO

"Do you have to get back to work right away?" Iris asked Luc as they stood on the front porch of the property they'd just given a thorough inspection.

Luc wrapped his arm around her waist and pulled her close. "What'd you have in mind?"

"I want to show you something." Iris smiled. "Something you *haven't* seen before."

"I like familiarity." He let her go and consulted the time on his phone. "I can take two hours. I've got Arnold covering lunch today."

"Great. Let's take a quick road trip. I want to show you a new restaurant I've read about. The photos looked interesting."

Half an hour later, as they cruised down crowded blocks of triple-deckers, insurance agencies and beauty salons, searching for a particular street number, Luc asked "How did you hear about this place? I thought I knew all the other restaurants on my turf."

"It's brand new. Didn't you see the write-up in the *Globe* last week?" Iris finally slowed down and pointed to an elegant storefront, painted black and wedged between a carpet outlet and a convenience store plastered with ads for Keno tickets and Western Union. "That must be it." She jockeyed her Jeep into a metered spot, the better part of a block away. "Let's see if we can get a table."

"This must be one of the last ungentrified sections of Somerville," Luc said as he eyed the rough-looking neighborhood. "I hope they've done their market research."

Chilled from the frigid air, Iris and Luc entered Café Six-One-Seven and were greeted with a welcome warmth and the din of excited diners crowded into a tiny space.

A young woman with a short gray bob and bright red lipstick asked, "Do you have a reservation? That's ok, I think we can fit you in." She led them to a tiny table, next to the kitchen.

Luc looked around. "This place is hopping."

"They've got buzz from being the new kid." Iris said, adding, "The food reviewer wasn't very impressed."

"You've brought me to a place with unimpressive food?" Luc studied the menu and let out a snort. "Seriously—"hand-glazed black cod filet"? I want to know how you're going to glaze it *without* using your hands. "Deconstructed pearl barley risotto with foraged mushrooms and succulent spinach compote"? *I'll* be the judge of whether the spinach is succulent. And the term "deconstructed" usually means that a sous-chef spilled something and reassembled it. Iris, my love, if I ever write pretentious horseshit like this please shoot me."

Iris lowered her head and shaded her eyes. "Now I remember why we rarely go out to eat. I need you to focus. I brought you here so we can check out what they've done with the interior design."

A hip-looking waiter filled their water glasses and rattled off the complicated specials. "Would you like me to send over the mixologist? We have some amusing craft cocktails."

Luc and Iris ordered the most fool-proof items on the menu and stuck with unamusing water to drink. She peered around to inspect the restaurant more closely. The walls were a glossy terra-cotta. Unfortunately, there were some landscape paintings hanging askew. Iris resisted the urge to get up immediately to straighten them, and instead adjusted her chair so that they were out of her peripheral vision. An ancient-looking black walnut hutch was positioned along a side wall with a potted gardenia on its counter, and a grab-bag of antique pendant lights hung from the ceiling.

"Forget about the pretentious menu. What do you think of the looks of this place?" Iris asked and watched Luc's reaction. "We've been talking about a clean California-modern vibe for the new place, similar to how the Paradise Café looks now, but what if we went for a rich patina like this, with layers and sensuality."

Luc leaned back in his chair as he looked around. "Reminds me of places I liked in Rome, but it's different from what I was imagining. We'd have to find the right building."

"Don't you think we just have? That was the best of all the properties we've seen all month."

"You really liked that place, didn't you? I admit it has potential, but it needs so much work."

"The work is mainly cosmetic. The structure is solid, other than the porch, which needs a new foundation. The windows are even in decent shape. I can see the rooms with deep colors and dark woods, maybe custom-designed sconces. We could even have an artist paint a mural on an accent wall. It would be like nothing else in the Boston area."

"Yeah, but that custom stuff takes a lot more time. You've also got the Harvard project. That's a lot of work for a one-woman-operation."

"The Harvard job is almost in the construction phase." Iris said. "After we get our approval tonight from the Historic Commission, I'll just be supervising. That should leave plenty of time to design and crack the whip on your renovation."

"I hope so. I'm a very demanding client." Luc winked. "Is tonight's approval a slam-dunk? You said that the commissioners could be picky."

Iris rubbed the back of her neck. "I'm a little nervous. You can never predict how the commission members will react." Gilles Broussard, the Harvard Dean who was effectively her client for the faculty guest house, had been texting her all morning to make sure that she was prepared for anything and everything with her presentation.

The waiter returned and, with a flourish, set down Luc's Rabbit Rigitoni and Iris' Tortellini en brodo. They focused on the food in front of them. After one bite, Luc shook his head sadly. "Store-bought pasta."

"Snob."

Luc spent the rest of the meal analyzing both of their entreés, parsing ingredients and passing judgment. After reassuring himself that the restaurant presented no threat to the Paradise Café, Luc ordered a pair of Espressos, then checked the time on his phone. "I should get back." He reached for his wallet.

Iris grabbed the check. "Let me get this."

"Thank you. Seeing this helps me imagine the new place with a different look. Let me think about it. I can't see it already done over, the way you can, but I trust your vision."

"The design needs to be as special as the food." She reached across the table for his hand and gave it a light squeeze.

When the waiter returned Iris' credit card, his laid-back

expression had taken on a worried look. Iris and Luc slipped on their jackets and wended their way through the tightly spaced tables to the door. As they stepped out into the weak winter sunlight, they saw flashing blue lights atop a police car racing toward them. The car double-parked and a beefy cop with a gray brush cut jumped out of the driver's side while his younger partner slid out of the passenger door.

Iris and Luc flattened themselves against the storefront so the police could get by them to wherever their emergency was.

Instead, the older cop approached her and asked, "Are you Iris Reid?"

When she nodded, he stated, "I'm placing you under arrest as an accomplice to a bank robbery. Drop the purse and put your hands on the police car."

Iris' heart raced. "A bank robbery? What are you talking about? This is a mistake."

Luc tried to get between them, his arms outstretched. "Leave her alone. You have the wrong person."

The younger cop shoved Luc away.

"Legs apart!" The older cop roughly patted Iris down, pulled her hands together behind her back, and snapped on plastic handcuffs.

"You're arresting me?" Iris felt dizzy with panic. She could see faces from inside the restaurant peering out at them. It was like a scene from a nightmare.

"Get in." The policeman nudged her toward his cruiser as his partner picked up her purse.

"I'll phone your brother," Luc shouted. "He'll straighten this out."

Iris looked back at him miserably. "Yes, please call Sterling! Have him come get me. Oh, and Sheba," she said, remembering her seven-year-old Bassett Hound, "Can you get to the house and let her out? She's been inside all day."

The tires squealed as the patrol car sped away.

CHAPTER THREE

The vinyl seat was low and smelled like a Burger King. The handcuffs cut into her wrists. Iris couldn't make out the unbroken stream of back-and-forth talk from the radio on the other side of the mesh cage.

On Sixth Street, she realized that the cops were taking her to Cambridge police headquarters even though they'd picked her up in Somerville. So the robbery must have happened in Cambridge. She leaned forward on her seat, placing her face close to the barrier. "Why do you think I was involved in this robbery? When did it happen?"

When they didn't answer, she tried another tact. "Talk to Detective Malone. He can vouch for me." She had helped Malone close a case the previous year. *Sure, he thinks I interfere with police business, but he knows I'm not a criminal.*

Brush Cut and his sidekick escorted Iris through the third floor squad room into a brightly lit interview room, then removed her cuffs. As soon as she was seated, Brush Cut gave her the full Miranda warning, ending with "Do you understand these rights?"

They still didn't explain why they had arrested *her*. The third floor was the major crimes department. She'd been in these interview rooms several times over the past year, but never as a suspect.

"Yes, I understand." Iris rubbed her wrists. "I want to call my lawyer."

"You'll get your chance," the officer called over his shoulder before the door slammed shut.

Iris spent the next ninety minutes racking her brains, trying to remember anything she might have done recently which could be construed as illegal, which might have linked her to this crime. There were, no doubt, minor traffic infractions, but, come on, this was Massachusetts. And they wouldn't have tied her to a bank robbery. *Sterling will fix this,* she kept telling herself. Her older brother, while stuffy and irritating, was a crackerjack attorney.

It was after four by the time her knight in shining wingtips strode through the door. He looked worried.

Iris jumped out of her seat. "Why do they think I'm involved in some robbery?"

Sterling lay his briefcase on the table and sat down. "There's a warrant out for you so all of your credit cards were flagged. A car that was used this morning in a bank robbery in East Cambridge was rented with a credit card in your name. The thieves got away with almost a million dollars."

Iris lowered herself into her seat, confused. "*My* credit

card?"

"The robbers shot a guard. He's in the ICU at Mass General and may not make it."

She let out a long, deep breath. "That's terrible, but with all the ID breaches around today any smart thief could have gotten a credit card in my name."

"A witness jotted down the plate number of the getaway car. Evidently Budget Rent-a-car at Logan Airport has video footage showing someone who looks a lot like you renting the car this morning. They also have a copy of your license and credit card on file."

"Someone who looks like me?" Iris' grip on the arms of her chair tightened.

"The police say the license matches the one they found in your purse, but they didn't see the Visa credit card that was used."

"I don't have a Visa card."

"Ever had one?"

"No."

Sterling took out a pen and legal pad from his briefcase. "Let's go through everything you did this morning."

"After breakfast at eight, I started drawing roofing details for the Harvard guesthouse project. In my office. Then I met Luc at eleven and we looked at a propperty for his new restaurant."

"Anyone see you before you met with Luc? A client or the

cleaning lady?"

"Only Sheba."

"Make any phone calls or send any e-mails?"

"Not while I was drawing. I worked from eight-thirty until ten of eleven, then walked over to meet Luc. We had lunch after that, then these cops accosted me as I was leaving the restaurant with Luc and treated me like I was Whitey Bulger. Wait—Gilles texted me several times this morning."

"Did you respond to him?

"No."

"Doesn't matter. You could have texted him back from the getaway car. The robbers were gone by ten."

"So they think I robbed a bank, then drove home to look at real estate with my boyfriend?"

Sterling took off his glasses and looked toward the window. "I know—it's crazy, but they must have some serious evidence. I agree that someone probably stole your identity and took out a credit card and duplicate license in your name. We need to see this tape to find out why they're so convinced that you were involved."

"You can get me out on bail while we straighten this out—right? I've got to present the Harvard project tonight at the Historical Commission. I've slaved over the design for six months. If these bureaucrats decide it doesn't fit the Harvard Square context, they can block the contractor from starting on schedule."

He looked at her solemnly. "I can't get you out of here that fast. The Middlesex County DA's office is charging you as an accomplice to a felony. If the guard dies, it's felony murder. Missing a meeting should be the least of your concerns."

"But...but Detective Malone can vouch for me. He can tell them I'm not a bank robber or a murderer."

"I have a call in to both Malone and the District Attorney's office."

Iris massaged her temples. "Would you please call my client to tell him that I won't be at the meeting tonight. Gilles is going to flip out. Don't say I'm in jail. Say I was in a car accident or something."

"Give me his number."

"And can you tell Ellie what's happened and have her take Sheba? I asked Luc to let Sheba out, but he has to work tonight."

Sterling wrote down their contact information. When he made the call to Gilles, Iris could hear squawking in the background as Sterling used his most soothing voice. When Sterling got through to Ellie, Iris grabbed the phone and explained the surreal circumstances herself. She couldn't answer most of her friend's questions.

Iris handed back the phone. "What do we do now?" She chewed her thumbnail, a habit she'd only recently broken.

"We wait." Sterling checked his phone for messages that

might have been left in the previous five minutes.

* * *

It was five p.m. by the time Detective Malone and Lieutenant Donna Choi of the Robbery Homicide Division joined Iris and Sterling in the now-crowded interview room. Malone refused to meet Iris' eye, staring instead at his cell phone, scrolling through messages. Lieutenant Choi, the one in charge of this case, was a whip-thin woman somewhere along the spectrum of middle age, her ebony hair rolled tightly into a bun. She looked like she could play a convincing game of poker.

After a few minutes, Malone mumbled something into Choi's ear and she cleared her throat. "The bank guard is being wheeled out of the ICU now. It looks like he's survived the surgery. Let's get down to business." She flicked on the recording machine and listed everyone present with their titles. "Ms. Reid, you were told your Miranda rights by the arresting officer, is that correct?"

"Yes."

"And you're answering these questions with your attorney present."

"Yes."

"Please go through everything you did today from the time you woke up to the time Officer Rudkowsky arrested you."

Iris detailed her day in all its prosaic innocence. When she was done, Choi reached into an envelope and slid a laminated card toward her. "Would you identify this?"

Iris studied it carefully. "It's my driver's license."

Sterling lifted a finger. "Have you checked to see if anyone's applied to Motor Vehicles for a replacement for this license?"

"We can look into that tomorrow," Choi answered. "Do you have a Visa credit card, Ms. Reid?"

"No."

"Never had one?" Choi raised an eyebrow.

"No. I have a Master Card and an Amex."

Choi passed her an official form and tapped a spot with her finger. "Do you recognize this signature?"

Iris stared at a car rental contract and spotted the forgery at the bottom. Someone had done a halfway-decent job of it. "My signature's very easy to copy because I print, but a handwriting expert will tell you that I didn't write this. I never make my 'R's like that."

The room was silent.

Sterling rolled a pen nervously between his fingers. "It seems to me that the only tie between Iris and this bank robbery is a forged rental form, a fraudulent credit card, and a replacement license. I think Detective Malone can speak for Iris' upstanding character."

Malone let out a self-conscious cough. "On several occasions Ms. Reid has provided invaluable help to the Cambridge P.D., even putting herself at risk."

Just as Iris' shoulders relaxed she heard Choi say, "Hmmm... risk. I heard the same word from a detective out in Lincoln when I made a few calls about Ms. Reid earlier. Evidently she was a suspect in a murder case last year." Choi waved her hand dismissively to head off any objection by Sterling. "Yes, I understand she was released," Choi continued, "but Lieutenant Gleason also mentioned that Ms. Reid put herself in jeopardy during the investigation. In my experience, people who are drawn to taking risks are often drawn to breaking rules. This is a serious crime, possibly murder. It wouldn't be the first time a seemingly respectable person got mixed up with the wrong crowd."

Lieutenant Choi leaned over and asked Malone, "Would you please run the car rental's surveillance tape?"

Malone pressed a button on the wall, the lights dimmed, and a projection panel lowered from the ceiling. Everyone slid their chairs around to face the screen, which came alive first as staticky snow and then, a few seconds later, with a view looking down at a woman standing at a counter—a woman who looked a lot like Iris, right down to the long dark brown hair, slightly aquiline nose, and even the red parka and black jeans that she now wore.

The tape ran for around five minutes during which time the

woman's face was seen from above in slight profile. After the woman filled out forms, and offered up a credit card and license, she turned toward the exit and looked directly into the camera. The shot froze. The police techs had enlarged her face and sharpened the focus.

Iris let out an involuntary whimper. *It was her own face looking back at her.*

CHAPTER FOUR

Sterling's parting words had been, "Someone's gone to a lot of effort to impersonate you, but you have a clean record and I should be able to get you out of here tomorrow morning after the bail hearing. Just get through tonight. Reids are tough." Iris sat on the hard lower bunk in the holding cell, trying not to cry. The room smelled of disinfectant with an undertone of urine.

She didn't feel tough at all. She wanted her dog. And her boyfriend.

Who was the woman on the tape and how had she managed to look so much like Iris? It had taken even Iris a minute or two to realize it wasn't her. And what did the imposter have against her, setting Iris up to get arrested?

When she didn't show up at the meeting tonight she was going to appear unprofessional, irresponsible. Would Gilles present the project or would he ask for a continuance, delaying the contractor's start date? And would her clients find out where she'd really spent the night? What would happen to the career she'd worked so hard to build?

After the detectives' exit from the Major Crimes' interview

room, she and Sterling had had an animated discussion. Then Lieutenant Choi had sent an officer from her division to escort Iris down to the bowels of the police station to book her. They'd fingerprinted her and taken mug shots. They even swabbed her cheek to keep her DNA for their records. She was assigned a number which was attached to a bracelet around her wrist. Her clothes were taken and replaced with a blue top and pants to be worn over stained prison-issue underwear. That was after the strip search which included all of her body cavities. Utterly humiliating.

Iris eyed the metal toilet in a corner of the holding cell. At least she had the room to herself.

No sooner had she thought this than the sound of multiple footsteps reverberated off the concrete floor in the hallway.

"You can't make me stay in here," a voice screeched. The cell door opened and a guard pushed a young woman inside. Her emaciated form collapsed onto the concrete floor, up against a wall, where she stared at Iris through large, vacant eyes.

"You got anything on you?" the woman demanded the minute the guard's footsteps receded.

"What? How could I? They searched me," Iris said.

"There's ways," the woman responded, wiping a runny nose on her blue prison-issue sleeve.

"I'm Iris."

"Crystal. Your first time?"

Iris nodded. That was the sum total of their small talk. The rest of the night degenerated in inverse proportion to Crystal's spasms, aches, and nausea. After a few hours of sleeplessness, the girl's sweating and vomiting escalated into agitated ranting. Iris tried to calm her with soothing words but got smacked in the eye by one of her flailing fists. Soon the girl was rolling back and forth on the floor. Iris had hung on as long as she could. She screamed for help.

A few minutes later, a guard's face appeared in the door's tiny window. She hauled Crystal away, leaving Iris curled up in a fetal position on a wafer-thin pallet trying to tune out the disgusting smells Crystal had left behind. Just before dawn, she dozed off.

In the morning, when she entered a Middlesex courthouse conference room, she could tell by Sterling's expression that the effects of her night-from-hell showed.

He pulled out a chair for her and placed a Starbucks coffee cup on the table. "Who gave you the shiner?"

"My junkie cellmate, finally dragged off to detox at four a.m. Please get me out of this nightmare." She gave her brother a desperate look, then pried the lid off the coffee and breathed in the warm aroma before taking a large sip.

"We're going before Judge Haggerty in half an hour. She should be sympathetic to our bail request. Then we can straighten out the rest of this." Sterling held up a Whole Foods shopping bag.

"I had Ellie pick out a suit and some make-up. Try to cover up the black eye."

"Is Ellie here?"

"Yes. So is Luc." Sterling left the room to let her change.

Ellie had included a hand mirror in the supplies and, thankfully, her own underwear. Iris did the best she could with make-up, but the purple bruise stood out against the exhausted pallor of her face. Iris felt steadier knowing that her friends had come, people who knew without a doubt that she was innocent of the charges.

When she was marched into the courtroom in handcuffs, she could see the stricken faces of her two friends sitting in the gallery. Their eyes widened as they registered her black eye.

The hearing itself went quickly. An attorney from the DA's office was there to voice her objections to bail, but Sterling made a strong counterargument. "This is a case of stolen identity. My client is a locally known architect with no record whatsoever. She's been falsely accused and has had to endure a night in a police holding cell where she was assaulted by her cellmate."

Sterling convinced Judge Haggerty that Iris was not a flight risk, and the judge set bail.

After Sterling made the arrangements to get Iris released, he led her toward a rear door. "We'll meet up with Ellie and Luc around the corner at Dunkin' Donuts. I need to warn you—this story has legs. The media's going to be all over it. Let me do the talking, OK?"

Iris nodded and lowered her head as they were met with a swarm of reporters. Someone thrust a microphone in her face.

"Iris, did you know your friends were going to shoot the guard?"

"Ms. Reid, what does Harvard have to say about your involvement in a murder-robbery?"

Among the shouting faces, Iris recognized her nemesis from college, Budge Buchanan, now a reporter for the *Boston Globe*. Even though she and Budge had reached an uneasy truce over the past year, she knew that his gloves would be off when it came to getting a scoop.

As Sterling repeated "No comment" and pushed through the crowd, Iris heard Budge shout "Iris, over here."

Iris fixed Budge with her most furious stink eye just as a blinding flash went off.

"Sorry," Budge gave her a wink. "Nothing personal."

That S.O.B. now had a "money shot" to go with his front page story for the next day's *Globe*.

CHAPTER FIVE

Iris evaded the reporters camped out in front of her house and fled to Luc's condo, where he whipped up her favorite lunch of spaghetti carbonara. She hardly tasted it. All she could focus on were the probable repercussions of her arrest, sure to be aired on that evening's news and in Tuesday's newspaper. Gilles would learn the real reason she hadn't been at the hearing, if he didn't know already.

Before leaving for the Café to prepare for the dinner crowd, Luc massaged her shoulders. "Why don't you take a nap? You look exhausted."

Iris longed to collapse onto a real bed, but first, she needed to do damage control. Gilles Broussard was the dean of Harvard's prestigious Graduate School of Design, and the one who had commissioned her to design a guesthouse for visiting faculty. He had encouraged her to design in her signature Neo-Modernist style—not a look guaranteed to win over the picky agency charged with protecting the City's historic fabric. Still, Iris had been careful to make the building fit in with its neighbors in proportions and materials. She was dying to know how the presentation had gone the previous night. But her call only got her as far as his fiercely protective assistant.

"Is Gilles available, Peg? I really need to find out what happened last night at the Historical Commission."

"He's tied up all afternoon in meetings, Professor Reid, but I can leave him a message." Peg, a woman in her sixties with an implausible shade of red hair, insisted on giving Iris that title after her one semester teaching a design studio.

"Do you know what happened? Was the project approved?"

Peg gave an irritated cough. Iris heard some shuffling of papers at the other end of the line. "You'd have to speak with the Dean about that. I'll tell him you called." Stonewalled.

Gilles was, no doubt, angry with her. She'd heard Sterling tell him that she'd been "unavoidably detained." That vague cover story had caused an outburst of panicked protest, barely intelligible in Gilles' French accent which intensified under stress, or at will.

She needed to unruffle his feathers. Pray God the commission had OK'd her design.

While Iris waited for Gilles to get back to her, Ellie dropped by the condo rolling a suitcase of Iris' clothes and leading Sheba on a leash.

"A crowd of reporters is swarming around your house." Ellie set down the dog bowl and water dish on Luc's kitchen floor. "They even took pictures of Sheba and me. I sure hope the police catch your imposter soon."

Amen, Iris thought.

She wandered around the condo but felt restless without her daily routine. Away from her office, she couldn't work on the last details for the guesthouse, and she didn't know if the Commission would require design changes. She decided to search the floor-to-ceiling living room bookcases for something to read. Luc had the usual assortment of guy books—biographies of presidents, books about wars, non-fiction. But he also had a respectable section on mysteries, and not just the shoot-'em-up CIA books. He had to be the most well-read chef/restaurant owner in the Boston area. She eventually settled on a John Le Carré mystery and curled up on the sofa with Sheba at her feet, determined to lose herself in the complicated plot. But her thoughts kept flitting to the woman who'd used her identity the previous day. How had she discovered their resemblance? Was she someone Iris knew?

As her eyes drifted shut, she pictured herself in a trench coat and large sunglasses, sitting behind the wheel of a gray Toyota, waiting, her fingers tapping to the bass notes of a Bruce Springsteen soundtrack. Iris barely stirred when Luc returned sometime around midnight and guided her into the bedroom.

* * *

The next morning, she was making a cappuccino with Luc's elaborate Italian espresso machine when he returned from the downstairs vestibule with the newspaper and unfolded it on the kitchen table. "Shit," he said.

Iris gasped when she saw the front page: a hideous head shot of her, black eye clearly visible, glared at the camera. The headline read: *Harvard Architect arrested in Cambridge Bank Robbery.* The byline was Budge's.

Harvard professor and architect Iris Reid, 44, pleaded not guilty to charges of driving the getaway car for the two men who shot a guard before escaping with $985,000. in Monday's bank robbery in East Cambridge.

The guard, Harry Snow, 37, father of four, is in critical condition at Mass General Hospital.

Lieutenant Donna Choi said that Reid is alleged to have rented a gray Toyota RAV 4 that was identified by witnesses as the one used by the bank robbers. Ms. Reid was tentatively identified as the driver. The SUV was later found abandoned in a driveway in Somerville.

Iris Reid is presently designing a guesthouse for visiting faculty of Harvard's Graduate School of Design. She taught at the School of Design last year and was involved in the Xander deWitt kidnapping case, ultimately helping the police capture deWitt.

Ms. Reid was released on $50,000 cash bail after her arraignment yesterday in Middlesex Superior Court.

The bank robbers, described as Caucasian males with Eastern European accents, remain at large. Anyone with information about this case should contact Detective Donna Choi at dchoi@cambridgepolice.org.

Pleaded not guilty. Iris' stomach lurched. Everyone who was ever arrested claimed they were not guilty, even if caught red-handed. Would her neighbors, colleagues, and clients believe she'd been involved in this?

Luc wrapped his arms around her. For a long moment Iris just stood holding on to him. She wiped her cheeks with the sleeve of her nightshirt and felt her anger building.

"I'm gonna kill Budge! Why did he have to bring up my ties to Harvard? They're going to fire me from the guesthouse project. I've already been caught up in one scandal. People were finally starting to forget about the deWitt thing. And now Gilles is going to know that I spent last night in a jail cell."

"You know the press: 'If it bleeds, it leads.'" Luc smoothed Iris' hair away from her face. "Budge will have to write the real story once the cops figure out the truth. Call Sterling. See what his investigator has dug up."

In a short telephone conversation, Sterling told Iris to meet him at his downtown office at two. In the meantime, Luc offered to drive her to the police impound yard in Inman Square to retrieve the Jeep.

They located the concrete bunker in front of a ten foot high chain-link fence surrounding captured cars and entered the overheated office. Behind a yellowing Plexiglas barrier, a bored-looking middle-aged woman with bright blue hair, sat reading a magazine. She looked up and regarded them through weary eyes. "Impound notice and driver's license."

Iris supplied these and the cashier peered at her computer screen, intent on something she saw there.

Iris held her breath, afraid that the woman might summon the police to rearrest her for something else. But instead, the cashier slid an invoice through the opening and intoned "$172.50 for the towing plus three day's storage."

"This is a mistake," Iris began. Then, seeing the woman's battle-scarred expression, she decided not to push her luck. She slid her credit card through the slot.

Iris and Luc followed arrows painted on the wall to a back door into the lot. The cashier buzzed them through. Outside, a skinny older man in an oversized parka was stamping his feet and blowing into his hands. He reached for Iris' paperwork and five minutes later they drove off in the liberated Jeep, now covered in a layer of grime. Iris dropped Luc at his car and headed back to the condo to get Sheba. She needed to get some fresh air. It was time for a brisk walk around Fresh Pond.

With Sheba's head out the passenger window, her ears flapping in the nippy late March breeze, Iris cruised past her own house. If anything, it looked like even more reporters were milling around on the brick sidewalk, flies drawn to a carcass.

She took a left onto Upland Road and drove two miles to their favorite walking site. She let Sheba out of the car and they headed over to the main path around the city's expansive, landscaped reservoir. After spending a night cooped up in jail and a whole day lying low inside Luc's condo, she appreciated being here even more than usual. And Sheba enjoyed her leash-free access to a dirt path shared by runners, dog walkers, cyclists, and other dogs. Iris loved eavesdropping on the conversations of Cambridge's quirky characters. This place was her version of *Mr. Roger's Neighborhood,* a friendly, all-accepting respite from reality.

They started out on their two-and-a-quarter mile circuit with Sheba pausing to sniff every enticing bush. While Iris waited for Sheba to catch up, tugging her wool cap down over her ears, she gazed through a chain-link fence at the dark surface of the reservoir. The breeze formed small whitecaps which made the surface shimmer. Clouds streaked across a crisp Titian-blue sky. She breathed in deeply. This place restored her soul.

Just as she turned to call Sheba, a familiar fellow dog walker approached, a 60-ish man with a silver ponytail who taught psychology at Harvard and owned a male Bassett Hound whom Sheba adored.

"How's Ringo today?" Iris called out.

The professor approached with a glint in his eye and rested a hand on Iris' arm. "You poor thing. This whole robbery thing—none of us believe you were mixed up in it." He studied her face expectantly, eyes hungry for some inside information.

Iris mumbled something about identity theft, clipped on Sheba's leash and tugged her away from the eagerly sniffing Ringo.

A usually friendly runner approached but didn't give Iris her customary wave, just stared fixedly ahead as she jogged past.

Iris fished out her big sunglasses from her pocket and kept her head down. She tugged again on Sheba's leash as they trotted back to the Jeep.

"Sorry, pup. We need to find a new place to walk until my notoriety dies down."

IRIS

CHAPTER SIX

Iris was too worried to eat lunch. Gilles still hadn't returned her call, and her attempts to reach his cell phone went straight to voicemail. She downed another cappuccino and prowled around Luc's three small rooms, Sheba trailing her anxiously. Iris visualized herself inflicting various slow and painful deaths on the thieves who'd used her identity to commit their crime. She needed to track these bastards down.

She checked her watch. It was time to drive downtown to meet with Sterling's investigator. Just as she was heading for the coat closet, Luc let himself in. "I got Arnold to cover lunch so I could go with you to the meeting. I don't need to be back until four." He cocked his head and smiled at her. "You might want to brush your hair."

Iris ran to look at herself in the bathroom mirror. Her thick, wavy hair stuck straight out making her look like a homeless, crazy lady. The bruise under her eye was a fraction lighter but now yellow was forming around the edges. She looked completely wrung out. She brushed her hair into submission and applied make-up under her eye, but the purple showed through. She smoothed on bright lipstick for distraction and slipped on her sunglasses. As she reached for her distinctive red parka on a hook in the vestibule she hesitated, then found a black wool coat that she'd left in Luc's closet to wear instead.

*   *   *

At Sterling's slick, corporate office overlooking Post Office Square, the receptionist led them to a conference room where Sterling was talking to a nondescript man about Iris' age and height. They both stood when Iris and Luc entered. Iris could see that the man's jacket strained along one side and wondered if he was wearing a shoulder holster.

Sterling made introductions. "This is Greg Peretti, our investigator. My sister, Iris Reid and her friend, Luc Cormier."

They sat and Iris forced herself not to accept the offer of more coffee. She was far too jumpy as it was.

Sterling opened a file and put on his glasses. "We have a trial date. It's in five months—July 14th. Between now and then, Greg will be gathering our own evidence. Hopefully, the police will find the thieves and dismiss the case before then. But we have to proceed by assuming they won't."

Peretti leaned forward in his seat. "Iris—can I call you Iris?—we need to figure out how these guys got their hands on your personal information. Have you lost or had your purse stolen recently?"

"Has your house been broken into, or your computer been hacked?"

"Anyone call trying to pull a phone scam on you?"

"Any of your mail gone missing?"

Iris answered no to each of his rapid-fire questions. "I even shred my personal papers before putting them into the trash."

"Is your mailbox secure—locked?"

"It's a slot through my door. But I don't get much mail anymore since I pay most of my bills online."

"A Visa card was taken out in your name."

Luc asked, "Where was it sent to?"

"You're the boyfriend—right? Some studio apartment in Somerville five weeks ago. The landlord said a woman claiming to be Iris Reid had rented the place on a month-to-month lease and paid first and last month's rent in cash up front."

"Somerville? The police found the abandoned robbery car in Somerville," Iris exclaimed, remembering every word of that damn *Globe* article.

"That doesn't narrow down our search," the investigator said. "The thieves might have picked Somerville for their drop site because no one knows them there, or they could have changed cars there for the same reason—because it was neutral territory."

"Were there any fingerprints left in the car?" Luc asked.

"None that gave the crime scene guys any hits. These rental cars never get fully cleaned so they're covered with random prints."

"But wouldn't the lack of Iris' prints on the steering wheel be significant?"

Peretti shrugged. "The DA will say she was wearing gloves. It's winter in New England. Everyone's wearing gloves."

"What about the fake driver's license?" Iris asked.

"A replacement for a stolen license—ironic, I know—was applied for and sent to the Somerville apartment as well," Peretti said. "They used your old photo so the woman who impersonated you must look a lot like you, but we knew that already from the rental car's surveillance tape. The landlady also described the woman who rented the apartment as fitting your general description, although the landlady thought the renter was around thirty years old."

Sterling broke in. "A man who'd been in the bank parking lot during the robbery was shown a picture of you after the police tracked down the rental car, and he said that you looked like the woman he saw waiting in the gray Toyota, but he couldn't be positive."

Iris' voice rose in frustration. "So, what can I do?"

"There are two issues here," Peretti explained. "The most

important one, obviously, is convincing the court that you weren't mixed up in the bank robbery. The second is restoring your credit from any damage these thieves might have caused. We're hoping for a break with the first issue—maybe some of the money the crooks stole will turn up and it can be traced back to them. Maybe one of the three will blab to a friend. But on the second issue: your credit reports should be monitored for irregular activity. Also, you'll need to file a police report and include it with letters to the three credit reporting agencies."

Iris looked wide-eyed at Greg. "You're saying I have to deal with the police again? I really don't want to do that."

"I'll go with you this time, babe." Luc squeezed her knee under the table.

She gave him a wan smile and turned to Sterling. "Isn't it enough to show the court that someone other than me had a credit card and replacement license in my name sent to this Somerville apartment?"

Sterling shrugged. "How can we prove you didn't orchestrate that? If you were planning on committing a crime, what better way to shift blame than to claim identity theft?"

Thanks, brother. Iris hated his smugness but knew that his unsentimental analysis was accurate.

CHAPTER SEVEN

Luc dropped Iris at his condo. He'd tried to cheer her up on the ride back, but she was too angry. The thieves hadn't been caught and the investigator didn't have any leads on the woman's identity. Greg's parting words were "Maybe we'll get lucky and they'll try to use your credit card again." Hardly a pro-active approach.

Sheba met her at the door and, as Iris slid down to the floor, her back against the entry wall, Sheba put her head in her mistress' lap. Iris ran her hand over and over the dog's coarse fur, over and over, her eyes closed.

When Sheba began to whine softly, Iris went to the refrigerator to find something for the dog's dinner. She grabbed some roasted chicken and, from the freezer, a bottle of Stolichnaya. After filling Sheba's bowl, she plunked several ice cubes into a tall glass and filled the rest with vodka, throwing in the withered remains of a quartered lime, not altogether green. It wasn't even five o'clock but, hell, it was happy hour somewhere. She took the bottle and the sweating glass back to the living room sofa and sipped her drink as she stared, unseeing, out the window at the buildings across the street.

How was she supposed to prove her innocence? The three criminals had scurried off to their hidey holes with the stolen cash. The police had a trail leading directly to her. The press had already convicted her. And the public viewed her with skepticism, if not fear.

The thought of returning to the police station, even to file a police report, terrified her. Spending Monday night in a holding cell had left a mark. She couldn't survive years in prison. The actual criminals would eat her alive.

The vodka warmed her insides. Had she eaten anything today? She rubbed her face absently and refilled her glass.

Later she awoke with a start. She was still in Luc's living room and the sky had started to darken. Her watch said six o'clock. She sat up and saw Sheba watching her attentively.

Iris fumbled for the remote on the coffee table and turned on the small flat screen in Luc's bookcase. A news announcer was talking about a worldwide conference on hunger being held in Geneva with shots of dignitaries from around the world shaking hands in front of a grand marble staircase.

Then the image changed to a different reporter, a man bundled in a hat and scarf, breath visible, standing in front of the Crimson Savings Bank, a banner beneath the picture reading 'Breaking News'. The reporter peered dramatically into the camera. "We've just had some tragic news. Harry Snow, the bank guard who was shot during Monday's robbery here in East Cambridge, has succumbed to his wounds. We learned from his doctors at Mass General that a single bullet had perforated his lungs. The wound became infected and Mr. Snow died today at 4:45 in the afternoon. Mr. Snow was thirty-seven, a husband, and father of four. The Cambridge detective in charge of the robbery case, Lieutenant Donna Choi, says the search for the robbers is ongoing."

As the news moved on to other stories, Iris punched off the remote and unsteadily refilled her glass.

CHAPTER EIGHT

The next morning, through the narrow slits between her eyelids, Iris could see bright, pulsing light. Her head was inside a cement mixer spinning round and round. She made it to the bathroom just in time to vomit violently, but with precision. She brushed her teeth, swallowed several aspirin, and staggered toward the kitchen where she found Luc sitting casually at the table reading the paper. Sheba eyed her from a spot at Luc's feet and hoovered up a piece of bacon from the floor.

"'Morning." Her voice sounded hoarse. "How come you're not at the market?"

Luc always got up at dawn to collect seafood and produce from his favorite purveyors. After delivering his haul to the restaurant's cold room, he'd usually sit at the café's mahogany bar with an espresso or two, planning the day's dinner menu.

"It's ten o'clock. I've gone and come back." He moved over to the espresso machine.

"Ten?" Iris fell into a chair, and reached down gingerly to pet Sheba.

"Judging by the vodka bottle, it looks like you had quite a

party last night. Sorry I missed it."

"Ugh, sorry. I swear I'll pull myself together. It's just that I saw on the news..."

"I know. The guard. Don't read the paper." He snatched it off the table and threw it in the trash bin. "You need to eat something. How 'bout toast to start?" He placed a large cappuccino in front of her and dropped two slices of sourdough bread into the toaster.

She stared at the mug. "Oh, god. I don't deserve you."

"True." He smiled, beat eggs in a bowl, and grated in some cheddar cheese.

She took a tentative sip of the coffee, then a gulp. Just as her vision began to gain focus, her cell phone on the table started up.

"Hello," she croaked.

"Irees." Gilles' unmistakable voice. "I know you've been trying to reach me, but I've been meeting with the Board about the guesthouse project. Since you didn't show up, I had to present it to the Commission and they want some design changes. I learned from the newspaper that you were absent because you'd been arrested in a murder-robbery case. I'm sorry to say that we all think it would be better if we gave the project to another architect to finish."

"But, Gilles—you can't do that. I would have been there on Monday night if the police hadn't arrested me by mistake. I shouldn't be penalized for that!"

"I'm sorry," Gilles cut her off, "but we can't have you drag the GSD into another scandal."

"I was just trying to help a student last year."

"Nonetheless, that scandal reflected negatively on Harvard."

"Gilles, this is my project. I've spent six months designing it. I passed on other projects in order to devote all my time to it."

"And we will pay you for your time. Our contract allows us to terminate for cause."

"It's not about the money or the legality. You know that."

"I'm sorry. It's out of my hands. The board has given the project to Vernon Elliott. He will be contacting you about transferring your CAD files."

"Not Elliott! You've got to be kidding me. He'll wreck my design."

But Gilles had already hung up.

Iris banged the table with her closed fist, then shook her hurt hand. "Fuck!" she screamed.

Sheba scrambled up from her spot under the table and padded over to stand behind Luc.

He slid a plate of eggs, bacon and toast in front of Iris. "That sucks, babe. But I've got another project for you. Bala called me last night and said that the sellers accepted my bid on that wreck of a property we saw on Sunday. I sure could use an architect."

CHAPTER NINE

Iris stirred the home-made vegetable soup in her bowl. The sharp edges of her mood were softening out the longer she sat in Ellie's warm, sunny kitchen. "Four days ago I was worried about a perky young yoga teacher who might want to snake my man. Since then, I've been accused of being a robber, thrown in jail, disgraced on the front page of the paper, and fired from my job."

"Luc's not going to trade you in. He adores you. But I can't believe Gilles gave your project to that dweeb, Vernon Elliott. Has the guy ever had an original thought in his life?" Ellie blew on her spoon. "Eat your soup. You look like you need the vitamins."

"I got the Commission's staff person to email me their decision," Iris said. "Those bureaucrats decided that there's too much glass on the front façade—the wankers. It makes me sick to think about what Elliott's half-assed alternative will be."

"Maybe your clients will realize the error of their decision once they see his design." Ellie broke off a piece of French bread, dragged it carefully through her soup and popped it into her mouth.

"Hey—do you have your copy of today's *Globe* handy? Luc wouldn't let me read it. I know there's something about me in it.

After he left for the Café, I tried to fish it out of the trash, but that sly dog took the front section with him. How bad is it?"

"I was wondering why you hadn't mentioned it." Ellie indicated with her chin the blue bin by the back door. "In recycling. There's nothing for Budge to say about the real criminals, so he's grinding out tabloid gossip about you."

Iris had made the front page again, if below the fold. At least they had dredged up a decent picture of her from her web-site this time. Budge had titled the article: **How to Read Iris Reid**.

Witty. Guess that Dartmouth education hadn't gone completely to waste.

Her neighbor, Alise, was quoted first.

I don't believe for a minute that Iris had anything to do with this. I've been her neighbor for sixteen years and I dog-sit for her sweet dog. Someone must have taken out a credit card in her name. She'd never be involved in this.

"That isn't so bad." Iris rose and refilled her bowl from the pan on the stove. She was suddenly ravenous. "Want some more?"

Ellie shook her head. "Keep reading."

Herbert Miller, a fellow Cambridge architect, pompous and lacking talent, had this to say:

I've seen Iris Reid around at architectural functions over the years. We've crossed paths, as one does in these tight professional circles. I've always found her to be stand-offish. I

wouldn't be surprised if she had a dark side.

"What an ass hole. I've never said a word to him."

"I think that's his point."

Iris read a few more quotes from acquaintances that varied from supportive, to prurient, to condemning. But when she reached the last paragraph, she let out a cry.

"Shit! How did Budge dig *him* up?"

"Everything's on the internet today. From your wedding announcement in the *Times* to Christopher's current linked-in contacts. Honey, there are no secrets in this modern age."

Iris forced herself to read the indictment by her ex-husband—the one she'd divorced thirteen years ago. The marriage had only lasted eleven months, so Iris figured it hardly counted. He'd moved to the West Coast as soon as the ink was dry on their divorce decree and she hadn't heard from the coke-snorting jerk since.

Iris Reid is a complicated woman. She's always been drawn to bad boys. We were briefly married when I was going through a troubled period, but I moved on. Sadly, it seems as if she has not.

Iris felt a flush seep up from the collar of her sweater, burning her cheeks. "The bastard! I'll kill him!"

"I can see why Luc didn't think you should read this." Ellie loaded the lunch things into the dishwasher.

Iris wadded the paper up into a ball and dumped it in

recycling. "Budge is dead, too."

"Deep breath, girl. We need to find these criminals before Budge can do any more damage to your character."

"What do you suggest?"

"Why don't you let the media know that you're dating Luc? *He's* certainly respectable. That way they can't imply that you're some kind of bank robbers' moll."

"I can't drag Luc into this. People might stop coming to his restaurant if they think he's involved with me. Besides, I don't want the press to know where I'm hiding out."

"OK. Let's try to figure out how the thieves could have gotten hold of your Social Security number and your mother's maiden name to apply for the credit card. Hell, I'm your best friend and even I don't know those things."

"It's not like I have my Social Security card lying out on a window sill or even in my wallet," Iris said. "I suppose someone could track down my mother's maiden name on the Internet if they were clever. Sterling's investigator asked if anyone had tampered with my mail or gotten access to my computer."

"And have they?"

"I haven't noticed any signs of a break-in, but we haven't had a regular mailman in several years, so no one would notice if a change of address form was submitted."

"What are you talking about?"

"The thieves might have gotten personal information from my mail if it was diverted to the Somerville apartment I told you about. They could have applied for the credit card using that information."

"Wouldn't you have noticed if you'd stopped getting mail?

"The Post Office only forwards first class letters, so the junk mail keeps coming. Since I pay my bills online, I hadn't registered until now that my mail's thinned out."

"It might be worth checking out that apartment. I wonder if there's anything left to see," Ellie said. "I can't imagine the thieves going back there again. And I'm sure that the police and Sterling's investigator—"

"Greg Peretti."

"—Peretti have combed over anything left behind."

"I guess it's a place to start. But I don't know how the criminals could have discovered any important data in my mail. Even credit card bills block out your full account number."

"Let me get my keys and we'll go check the place out. And on the way, I want to hear more about little Ms. Yoga."

CHAPTER TEN

The apartment was in East Somerville, far from the hipster-haven of Davis Square. Ellie slowed down as they cruised past the small brick apartment building next to Depasquales Funeral Parlor. She parked a block away and Iris pumped some quarters into the parking meter. They circled back on foot, keeping an eye out for anyone who might be watching the building. On the way over they'd been too busy discussing Yoga Girl to come up with a plan of entry.

Greg Peretti had given Iris the Apartment number: 1-D. They entered a dim vestibule. The aluminum mail box for 1-D had an identifying name tag, *Reid, I.* "What nerve!" Iris marched over to the inner door. They waited several minutes, hoping that someone would pass through and leave it open long enough to grab. Finally, Iris fished a library card out of her wallet.

Ellie stared at her. "We can't just break and enter. You're out on bail, remember? Why don't we ask the Super to let us in?"

"Technically, I rented this apartment, so it's not illegal for me to go in. I just don't happen to have my key with me."

"I wonder why not." Ellie gave her a disapproving look.

"We're trying to prove that you're *not* the one who rented this apartment."

Iris slid her card down the gap between door and jamb in one smooth sweep and the door popped open. "I do this all the time when I forget my key to a building site."

"That's not something you'd want to advertise on your web site." Ellie followed her past an open staircase to the rear of the corridor.

Iris repeated her library card trick and the door to 1-D opened to reveal an almost bare apartment. A card table and a wooden chair with one missing rung on the back sat by the lone window in an open studio.

"How could anyone think that an architect would rent this dump?" Iris walked over to inspect a cheap, aluminum teapot on the stove in the kitchenette. What looked like white powder coated the handle.

"The crime-scene guys have been here. Since my fingerprints are now in the system, the police will see that mine don't match the ones they find here." Iris looked around. "This place is totally depressing."

"Your doppelgänger probably stayed just long enough to read her mail."

"You mean *my* mail."

Ellie rummaged through the two kitchen cabinets and held up a box. "She drinks Lipton's Tea. That should narrow down our search."

"Funny." Iris dragged the chair over to a closet and climbed up to feel around on a high shelf. "I don't know what I expect to find here. The police have already checked this place out and Peretti said he found nothing."

"This place is the only tie we have to the bank robbers." Ellie let out a long breath. "It's our only lead."

Iris felt the chair seat beneath her sag just before she lost her balance and crashed to the floor.

Ellie ran over. "Are you OK?"

"Just swell—some more bruises to go with my black eye." Iris scowled at the broken chair leg and rubbed her shin. "The damn thing was booby-trapped." She looked up to see a skinny young man with a bad case of acne standing at the open door, staring down at her.

"What are you doing here?" he said.

Iris tried to get up with some dignity. "I rent this studio."

"No, you don't," he said.

"Who are you?" Iris countered.

"1-C. And you're not the girl who lives here."

"I pay the rent."

He looked dubious. "You're the mother?"

"I am *not* the mother." Iris waved him in. "Get in here, 1-C. Tell me about the woman who's been staying here."

"Why should I tell you anything? You're not the cops."

Ellie caught Iris' eye. "Tell him the truth."

"Don't you read the papers? Doesn't my face look familiar?" Iris asked. "The woman who rented this place stole my identity. She used a credit card with my name to rent the getaway car that was used in a bank robbery."

The man's mouth dropped open. "Oh, my God. You're that mean-looking bank robber?" 1-C started to back away.

"No! I'm trying to find the real robber so I can clear my name."

"You mean the girl I saw was the *real* bank robber? She lived right next to me? This is so cool." 1-C stepped inside and closed the door, his wary expression changing to conspiratorial. "I just saw her one time. About a month ago. I was going out just as her door opened. I noticed her because she was a total babe."

"Did the police ask you about her," Iris asked. "Or an investigator?"

"No, no one's contacted me, but I work strange hours."

Iris could feel goosebumps on her arms. This guy had seen the imposter. Iris could nail the bitch. "Describe her."

"About your height. My age. A lot of long hair, dark brown like yours, but," he paused in thought, "there was something weird about the hair."

"Weird—how?" Ellie asked.

"I'm a make-up artist. Jeffrey Gardner, by the way. I work next door at Depasquales."

Iris and Ellie's eyes widened when they registered that 1-C worked with corpses at the funeral home next door.

He gazed out the window with unseeing eyes. "Now that I think about it, her hair didn't sit right. It might have been a wig."

Ellie tilted her head. "As a make-up artist you must study faces. What were her features like?"

"She had beautiful skin. White, but like a pearl, lustrous. Granted, most of my clients have waxy skin by the time I work on them. She had sunglasses on so I didn't see her eyes." He squinted as he examined Iris' face. "She looked very much like you, similar nose, same bone structure, except you're a lot older. And your skin doesn't have that pearly look."

She glared at him. "Did she speak? Any accent?"

"She didn't say a word. She was rushing out the front door and barely noticed me."

"Did you see where she went? To a car or on foot?"

"You better believe I watched her go. She strapped on a

helmet and got on an old silver motorcycle parked in front of the building. She was one bitchin' babe."

Iris and Ellie both leaned forward and, at the same time, said, "And?"

"She zoomed off." Jeffrey shrugged.

"Did you notice the license number?" Iris asked hopefully.

"I'm good with visual stuff," he pushed the hair out of his eyes. "But numbers, not so much."

The two women exchanged frustrated glances.

"If it helps, I did notice that her ride was a Honda."

CHAPTER 11

Once they were back in Ellie's car, Iris used her cell phone to call Greg Peretti and filled him in on the afternoon's discoveries.

"Jeffrey Gardner in 1-C? I've been trying to track him down." Peretti's tinny voice came over the speakerphone. "Good work. I'll let the cops know he needs to be interviewed and they can send a sketch artist over. If this guy is willing to testify that you weren't the woman staying in 1-D, we're halfway to convincing a judge that you were set up."

"Can we can track this person down now that we know she drives a silver Honda motorcycle?" Iris asked.

"It's worth a try, but I'm sure there are a lot of those bikes around and she might live in New Hampshire, Rhode Island, or who knows where. I wish the guy was bike-savvy enough to give us a model number. Still, it's a great lead. I may have to put you gals on the payroll."

"Gals?" Ellie mouthed silently before pulling on the handbrake in front of Luc's condo.

*   *   *

Ten minutes later, Iris was peering at her skin in the bathroom mirror. It looked puffy from the impressive amount of vodka she'd consumed the previous night. Her face had a dull, haggard look. No wonder 1-C thought she could be the age of a grown woman's mother. She slapped on some moisturizer. She'd go to the dojo for a sparring session, get her blood circulating. But first, she needed to take care of some business.

Sitting on the living room sofa, her phone in her lap, she leafed through the "Contractors" section of her black leather address book. She punched in the direct number for the principal of a large local company she'd worked with many times.

"Butch, it's Iris Reid."

"Iris. How are you holding up? I've been reading a lot of nonsense about you in the newspaper." Butch's voice dripped with false solicitude. Most contractors thought architects were too full of themselves, so one getting taken down a peg was a source of amusement.

"It's all under control." Iris said evenly. "I've got a project I'm fast-tracking. A new restaurant in a crazy old house on Mass. Ave. I could probably have drawings done in a few weeks and we'd need to break ground in May. Would you guys be interested?"

"Gee, we're awfully busy this Spring. We've got a waiting list of at least six months. Maybe if we'd had more notice. Try us next time."

Iris worked her way through seven contractors, starting with the larger firms which had the manpower to take on a project on short notice. After seven rejections she began to suspect that Cambridge's robust building industry was not the problem. These guys didn't want to be associated with a suspected murderer.

It was too much. First, her Harvard design commission got handed over to some second-rate hack. Now, she couldn't even dig up workers for Luc's restaurant renovation. Her own boyfriend might be forced to use someone else to get his job done. How much humiliation could she take?

She looked over at Sheba, splayed indecorously on her back and snoring happily at the other end of the sofa. Iris slid over and rubbed her dog's belly. Sheba slept on. Something tugged at Iris' memory and she reached for her phone.

"Ellie, didn't you tell me that your cleaning lady's nephew just got his General Contractor's license? What do you know about him?"

CHAPTER 12

Rosica Bakalov felt disoriented having her evenings to herself, even four months after her "career change". She ran a hand through her short, reddish-blond hair as she lay back on the living room couch in the family's modest East Cambridge home. She missed the camaraderie with the other girls, even that bitch Juelle. They'd hang out in the Central Square Dunkin Donuts before their shifts started, making comments about the Johns. What do they call that? Trench humor.

Rosica was the queen of hand jobs. She would have bet that her regulars missed her. But the pain in her wrist was, apparently, the onset of carpal tunnel syndrome. Ever resourceful, Rosica had come up with a brilliant new source of income: stealing IDs to sell on the dark web from computers donated to a church which happened to have a pliable, dishonest assistant. But the money coming in wasn't fast or abundant enough to ward off the bank's foreclosure notices on their house.

Mama came up with the idea of robbing the bank that held their mortgage. She liked the irony. Rosica knew it would be a mistake, on more levels than she cared to count. Relying on her brothers, especially that hothead Georgi, to work as a team was bound to fail. And escalating their illicit activities to the level of a grand larceny was pushing their skill sets. But Mama would not back down. So they robbed the bank and Georgi shot the guard. Still, thanks to Rosica and her clever use of the Reid woman as a red herring, the cops hadn't been able to pick up their trail.

She roused herself from her musings and wandered into the kitchen to refresh her customary cocktail of rum-and-Diet Coke then reparked herself on the sofa facing an enormous flat-screen that Georgi had gotten "off the back of a truck". Images of heavily-made-up housewives with fake tans played across the screen. *She could be one of those bitches up there if she had the money to dress like they did.* Off-screen, she bet they wore pink sweats with *Victoria's Secret* across the butt like the ones she had on now. Rosica cocked her head, listening for sounds from her Mama's bedroom, directly overhead.

Mama used to be good at devising plans. She was the one who'd worked the blackmail scheme which had financed the family's exodus from Bulgaria four years earlier. She'd told U.S. Immigration that they would all be killed if they went back to Sofia (perfectly true, though not for the reasons she gave). That had eventually scored them all green cards. For that performance alone her children owed her, despite her continued relish in using scathing invictive to make her three grown children feel spineless and ashamed. Georgi had fallen into disgrace after stupidly shooting the guard and was now holed up at his girlfriend's apartment to avoid any more of Mama's lectures. The burden had fallen on Rosica and Drago to pick up the slack after Mama's exhausted hospice worker left at three each afternoon.

Rosica, the youngest and smartest of the three siblings, had been twenty when they'd all emigrated. She'd spent her days inhaling hazardous fumes at a Somerville dry cleaners and her nights at free classes learning English, with side lessons in computer hacking from a Bulgarian guy she knew. Unlike her brothers, she'd managed to erase pretty much all traces of her Eastern European accent.

Mama had put down the balance of her money from the blackmail scam as a deposit on this house in East Cambridge right before the real estate market went crazy. But the Crimson Savings Bank, just as smart as the old lady, cranked up their adjustable mortgage rate every six months until the monthly payment outstripped what she and her brothers could scrape together.

The kitchen door slammed and heavy footsteps headed toward the refrigerator. Rosica heard the predictable snap of a pull-top and turned to see Drago standing in the living room archway eyeing her above a dripping can of Bud Lite.

Her brother was a handsome man. With his square jaw, black slicked-back hair, and gleaming gold neck chain, he would be the picture of a successful man in the old country. He would already have a pretty wife at his side and a bunch of kids. But here he worked as a truck driver, delivering heavy cases to liquor stores all day. His hard eyes warned off all but the dimmest of girlfriends. Then again, he seemed to prefer them stupid.

Drago put the beer down on a table by the entry, pulled out a pack of unfiltered Camels from his leather bomber jacket, and lit one. He rifled through the day's mail. "You bring her dinner?" he asked through his teeth.

"Go check yourself. But don't smoke in her room. And bring down the tray." Rosica sipped from her drink, then went back to the figures she was tallying on a pad. Her nearby laptop showed images of houses from a Miami real estate broker.

Two hundred and eighty-six thousand dollars of the money they'd stolen had erased their mortgage. The remaining balance of their haul would be divided four ways. After paying a lawyer to process the closing without asking embarrassing questions, they'd each get one hundred and seventy-two thousand dollars, enough to put hefty deposits down on their own places. There was only one problem. Georgi had turned the duffle bag holding the money over to Mama and she wouldn't give it back. She said it would draw too much attention if the family made major purchases at the same time so she doled out a hundred dollars at a time. They could have taken the money, even Mama's share since she wouldn't need it to live on for much longer, but if they did that, she would put a curse on them, and that was one thing they couldn't risk.

Mama had come up with the concept, but it was Rosica who had used her electronic skills to hack into that Reid woman's computer to rent the Somerville apartment where the credit card and license were sent, and to dress up like Iris Reid to hide their real identities during the robbery. Drago and Georgi had supplied the brawn but, even then, Georgi had screwed up.

So Rosica considered that this next step would be hers alone. She still had Iris's hard drive. Mama had warned her not to push her luck, but the stupid woman's bank information was just sitting there, calling out to Rosica.

How much money did Iris Reid keep in her savings account?

CHAPTER 13

On Friday morning Iris double-checked her GPS and turned onto Maple Street in nearby Watertown. She searched without success for the telltale pickup trucks and dumpsters that signaled a construction site. After double-checking the house number, she pulled into the driveway of a modest Cape on a tiny lot. A lone motorcycle was tipped on its side stand close to the attached garage. If this little operation was the scale of the work Milo Miller took on, then maybe he wasn't the right guy for Luc's complicated project.

Newly curious about motorcycles, Iris examined this one—a bright blue BMW. She had never noticed before how sleek and ergonomic they could be. This one was a beauty.

She stood on the stoop, poised to ring the doorbell. She needed to find a crackerjack contractor. Luc was counting on her to pull off the look she had sold him on for his restaurant and the work would require a high level of craftsmanship. She hesitated, almost deciding to leave, when she heard the high-pitch whine of a power saw coming from the back of the house.

What the hell. I'm here. She let herself in through the

unlocked front door and followed the sound resembling a dentist's drill to the kitchen. She could smell the dried coffee scent of freshly-cut wood, and she saw in profile a slim-but-muscular guy hunched over a biscuit joiner. He didn't look like any contractor she'd ever seen. He had a jet black braid down the middle of his back and wore black leather pants. A complicated tattoo spiraled down one muscled arm below his black t-shirt sleeve. A tool belt slung low on his narrow hips was the only concession she could see to his trade.

"Hello," she screamed to make herself heard.

He turned and slid his safety goggles to the top of his head. "Hi—you must be Iris. Sorry I didn't hear the bell. I'm Milo." His voice was soft. He gave her a slight smile and extended his hand.

Silver-colored eyes, rimmed with thick black lashes, stared at her from a height two or three inches taller than her own five-foot-eight. He looked to be in his early thirties. She had trouble taking her eyes off of his sensuous, bow-shaped mouth, but gave herself a mental shake. "Where's the rest of your crew? Are they on a break?"

"Several of my guys are finishing up another job so I'm here on my own."

Iris walked over to the cabinet boxes neatly lining two walls with gaps left for appliances. She squatted to look at the mortise-and-tenon joints, then ran her hand over the tightly-grained wood.

"Is this black walnut?"

Milo looked a little sheepish. "I know. Pretty extravagant, huh? A friend from Vermont got his hands on a load and I bought the lot. Figured I'd do it right in my own kitchen."

Now it made sense. This was his place. She liked what she saw of his carpentry skills, but could he manage a team of sub-contractors? He didn't exactly exude authority.

"Countertop?" she asked him.

"Calacatta marble with a matching slab used as the backsplash up the wall," he responded.

"That'll be a nice balance with the walnut."

They sat on a makeshift bench and discussed his experience and background. He told her about other G.C.s he'd trained with, and asked intelligent questions about Luc's project. Forty minutes later, clutching a list of his references, Iris got up to leave, hoping she'd found her new contractor.

CHAPTER 14

It was time to return to her own house. As much as Iris loved spending time with Luc, she needed to work on his project in her home office, sketching at her drafting table. She had also run out of clean clothes and needed to go through her mail.

She collected Sheba and her rolling suitcase from Luc's condo and texted him from the rickety cage elevator to come join her after work.

Iris was relieved to find no reporters laying siege on her sidewalk, but she still parked a few houses away so as not to announce that she was back. She and Sheba jogged through her gate to the kitchen door which was screened from the sidewalk by a tall fence.

She threw her car keys on the counter and noticed her next door neighbor, Alise, watering her African violet collection on her windowsills. They exchanged waves. Iris turned up the thermostat on her way to the front hall to retrieve the letters that had been pushed through the mail slot. She collected the *Globes* stacked up on her front porch and dumped them directly into the recycling bin. As she separated bills, magazines and junk mail into piles on the kitchen island, she noticed the voicemail light blinking on her home phone. The start of the first message stopped her half-way through tearing open an envelope.

"Ms. Reid, this is Anita McBride from the Crimson Savings Bank. Would you please call me at 617-432-4893 as soon as possible? Thank you."

Iris reached the Branch Bank Manager on the second ring.

"Thank you for returning my call. I wanted to be sure you understood that by liquidating your savings account the other day you're no longer be eligible for the fee waiver on your checking account. You will be charged $12.95 a month for our basic checking tier. Were you aware of that?"

A moment's silence, then Iris answered, "I haven't withdrawn any money from my savings account."

Iris heard some tapping on keys, then Anita's voice came back on. "Two days ago $97,862. was transferred out of your account. Are you saying that you didn't make this transaction?"

"Yes, I mean no, I didn't touch my savings account!" Panic rose in Iris' chest. "Where was the money transferred to?"

"It was wire-transferred via your web account to an account in your name at Fidelity. Your correct login and password were used. The Fidelity account is: X19-769342. Is that yours?"

"I don't have an account there. You need to get it back! Call Fidelity right away before the thieves can move it again." Her voice was too loud to be polite.

"Oh, dear. I'm going to have to refer this matter to our legal department. Someone from the bank will call you back shortly." *Click.*

Iris was shaking as she set down the receiver. Someone was reaching into her life, helping themselves to anything they wanted. What would they take next?

Sheba growled softly.

Iris had inherited a vintage Porsche the year before from a crazy client who was now dead. After a few blow-out rides on Route Two, at a speed well above the posted limit, she'd decided that the car was too impractical to keep. She'd sold it to the manager of the Mobil station where her Cherokee was serviced and had planned to use the proceeds to replace her ancient Jeep and to pay down her scary mortgage.

Should she report this to the police? Would they help her or think she was faking more evidence of her alleged identity theft? She needed someone on her side—a combination of Columbo and

Rambo. She reached for her cell phone and punched in Greg Peretti's number.

Iris' words came out in a rush, and she barely breathed as she waited for his response. Peretti would know how to get her money back quickly. Seconds ticked by.

Finally he said, "You'll need to file a police report. I know this is hard to hear but this theft actually strengthens your case for identity fraud."

She groaned. "That's it? That's your advice—to be philosophical about having my whole savings wiped out?"

"Give me the Fidelity Account number and I'll find out if the money's still there. It's probably in Eastern Europe by now but let's see if they've left any breadcrumbs to follow."

CHAPTER 15

Iris drifted awake the next morning with the vague sense that something terrible had happened. She reached over for Luc's comforting body but felt only the cool, empty duvet. She lay blinking in the dim light, trying to remember. Then she did. A small whimper rose from the back of her throat.

She grabbed for her cellphone on the nightstand. Luc had responded to her text from the night before: *I'm beat, Babe. Let's catch up tomorrow.*

Was he starting to distance himself from her? Who could blame him if he was? She was such a loser. Luc had his own reputation to think about. He'd invested everything in his restaurant and didn't need his association with her to jeopardize its success. He could find a woman with a whole lot less baggage. Maybe a certain younger yoga instructor.

She squeezed her eyes shut. She loved Luc. It had taken her so long to find him. After all those years of nightmare dates and the ill-advised marriage that had shaken her confidence, she had finally opened up to a guy. Now she'd probably lose him and be alone forever.

Iris shrugged out of the flannel nightgown (that she'd never worn in front of Luc) and into the shower. The hot water pounded over her until her tears stopped and a rising anger took their place. She toweled off and shook her head like a wet dog to clear the water from her ears.

Dammit— I'm going to get my life back.

She threw on a pair of jeans and a baggy old sweater before descending to the kitchen. Weak sunlight slanted in through the mullioned windows, leaving faint rectangles on the marble kitchen table.

After her second cappuccino, Iris uncapped a pen with her teeth and printed on a pad of paper: *How did thieves get my personal info?*

Then she crossed out the last two words and wrote: *How did thieves get my savings account number?*

This had gone beyond knowledge of her Social Security number or her mother's maiden name. There were no signs of a break-in at her house and her bank card hadn't been stolen. She often did her banking on-line, but her computer was password-protected. She'd gotten Elvis, a particularly tech-savvy student from Harvard's GSD, where she'd taught the previous Fall, to help set up her new computer over Christmas break. While he was installing anti-virus software, he'd urged her to change her passwords to something harder to hack than her dog's name. Then he made her memorize it instead of keeping it in her desk drawer in a file cleverly labeled "passwords". She had done all that. So how had someone hacked into her account?

She checked her watch. It was nine-thirty on Saturday morning. That was late enough in the day to call a graduate student, wasn't it?

When he answered she could tell that, evidently, it wasn't.

"Professor Reid?" answered a sleep-soaked voice.

Once she had explained what had happened, Elvis was wide awake. He seemed to take it as a personal affront that a hacker could have breached the firewalls he had set up. Twenty minutes later he was at her front door, chaining his bicycle to the corner column of her porch.

Elvis spent the next half hour tapping and frowning at her computer, fingers flying over the keyboard, muttering to himself, and drinking the successive cups of espresso that Iris kept supplying next to his mouse. Periodically he pursed his lips to blow his straight black bangs out of his eyes.

Finally, Elvis tilted back in his chair, folded his arms, and looked smug. "No one has breached this puppy's fire walls."

Iris stared at him. "But how did they move money from my savings to another account?"

"That information's above my pay grade. But the data didn't come from this computer." Elvis stood and shrugged into the down parka he had tossed on the floor next to his chair.

Iris held up her hands, stalling him. "Where else could the thieves have gotten my savings account number?"

Elvis shrugged. "Well...what did you do with your old computer?"

CHAPTER 16

Iris spent the next twenty minutes searching through old e-mails before she called Ellie. "Do you still have the e-mail you sent me with the name of the church that picked up my old computer?"

"You're doing your taxes already? Didn't they leave you a receipt?"

"I can't find one. I've cleaned out my computer trash folder recently so I don't have anything. You keep all your old e-mails. Can I come over? It's important."

Iris hurried the block-and-a-half to Ellie's house through the slushy late-March streets to find her friend waiting at the front bay window. Ellie brandished a print-out. "I found it in the archives of the neighborhood list server. The church was collecting old computers to send to Africa. But I doubt your ancient desktop will be worth much of a deduction."

Iris scanned the notice as she followed Ellie back to the kitchen. *"The Church of the Little Lamb in Watertown is looking for used computers. We will pick up your old monitors, CPUs, and keyboards, erase all personal information from the hard drives and send them to a school we support in Mozambique. Call 617-492-*

7822 for a pick-up time and a receipt for tax purposes.

"I wonder..." Iris dropped into a seat at the kitchen table and rubbed her lower lip between her fingers.

Ellie leaned forward in her seat. "You wonder what?"

"My savings account was cleaned out yesterday—"

Ellie stared at her without blinking. "And you're telling me this now?"

"Sorry, I was too upset when the bank called. The jerks who stole my identity must have decided that setting me up for the bank robbery wasn't enough."

"Is the bank going to cover the loss? You had the Porsche money in there, didn't you?"

"The Crimson Savings bank manager called me back after checking with their legal department. She said they needed to learn the verdict from my criminal investigation before discussing what would happen with my account."

"This would have to happen at the same bank that you're accused of robbing. As if you didn't have enough pressure. "

Iris stared at the picture of a shepherd and his flock of sleepy-looking sheep on the flyer. "I've been trying to figure out how the thieves could have known my bank account number. It finally dawned on me that I had all kinds of financial information on my computer, so I had Elvis come to check it this morning. He ran it through all kinds of tests but is sure that it hasn't been hacked. Then I remembered my old machine. They could have gotten my information off that."

"Wow. So you think the church drive was a scam?"

"Think about it. It's the perfect set-up. How would anyone know if they ever erased all your data from the hard drive?"

Ellie tucked some curls of red hair behind an ear. "This is a twenty-first century nightmare. Our whole lives are on these machines and they need to be replaced every five years. And it's almost impossible for a normal person to know how to strip down the hard drives."

"I did erase everything I thought was sensitive—all my bill-paying information. I even cleared my cookies and browsing history. But I learned from Elvis that savvy hackers can still find that stuff on your hard drive."

Ellie grabbled in her purse for her keys. "We need to go check out this church." She paused then sat down again. "Wait— shouldn't we call that investigator from Sterling's office? It could be dangerous if we run into the thieves."

Iris frowned. "I already talked to Greg Peretti. I get the impression he does most of his investigating from the safety of his office chair. Besides, I want to see these bastards for myself. I want to rip the wig off this wanna-be Iris Reid with the porcelain skin."

"Stand down, girl. We don't even know if this church *is* connected to the scam. But if it is, the bad guys might recognize you from the fake license, or hell, they might have even looked through your old vacation photos. You need a disguise."

Ten minutes later, Iris came out of the master bathroom in a paisley polyester dress that Ellie had found months before at the Garment District, a local vintage clothing store, for a costume party. Ellie handed her some cat's eye glasses from the top of her bureau and peered at Iris. "Needs one more thing. Follow me."

Raven's room was a mess. Ellie's daughter had left several large, colorful canvasses of her paintings stacked against one wall and clothes strewn in a layer all over the floor. Ellie rummaged through a cardboard box in Raven's closet.

"How is my goddaughter enjoying herself in Barcelona?" Iris asked. "It's been weeks since I got her last postcard."

Ellie handed Iris a blond wig. "Mack and I think this college year abroad business is really just a *tinder* hunting ground. All I hear about in her texts are 'Alejandro-this' and 'Santiago-that.' She hasn't sent us any pictures of new paintings."

"Oh, those college years..." Iris stepped into Raven's bathroom. She pulled on the wig, added the glasses, and checked the effect in the mirror. "Everything's blurry through these. You must be blind."

"Aren't they great? I got them at the Garment District too. I've been meaning to get the lenses changed to my prescription."

"Do I look like I'm wearing a disguise?" Iris followed Ellie down the ornate Victorian staircase.

Ellie reached into a basket by her front door and lifted out a fuzzy cap. "Here, wear this over the wig and you'll look fine."

Iris figured she probably looked no more eccentric than most typical Cantabridgeans.

They took Ellie's car, and its GPS directed them to a side street between Watertown's two main drags, Mt. Auburn Street and Arsenal Street. Wedged between a seedy-looking florist and a greasy-spoon diner was a boxy, two-story stucco building with a lit-up sign over the front door: *Church of the Little Lamb.*

Inside, past a vestibule, was a small waiting area with an orange plaid sofa and a few grey plastic chairs. A beat-up desk stood in an alcove to the right. There, behind a computer, sat a pale young woman with short blond hair that looked like she cut it herself. She peered up at them through thick glasses and said in a soft voice, "Welcome. My name is Helen."

Ellie held up a finger. "May I use your Ladies' room?"

"Certainly." Helen gestured to a door. "First door on your right." She turned to Iris. "Can I help you?"

Iris glanced at the computer to see if it looked familiar, then smiled back. "I sure hope so, Helen. My name is Anna Brewster. I donated my old computer to your church back around Christmas and it turns out that I left some important information on it that I now need for my taxes. I'm really hoping that it hasn't already been sent to Africa."

Helen's pale eyes rounded. "Oh, dear. All the computers we picked up in December went into a container bound for Mozambique. We had such a gratifying turn-out before Christmas that the whole container filled quickly. The schools are so appreciative. The children there have so little."

Iris leaned forward on the desk. "Is there any chance that not all the computers fit in the container and that mine might still be here waiting for the next shipment? I'd be so grateful if you could check."

Helen looked at her dubiously just as Ellie came back through the door followed by a thin, freckled man in his mid-forties dressed in pleated khakis and a sweater vest over his blue oxford shirt.

"Here's Pastor Bob. He keeps the inventory list." Helen looked at the man reverentially. "Mrs. Brewster donated a computer in December and is wondering if it might still be here."

Iris had hoped to sound less direct. "It's such a wonderful, charitable project you're doing. I'm sorry to be a nuisance. If it wasn't so difficult to duplicate this information I need for my taxes I wouldn't bother you."

"No bother. Why don't you come with me back to my office. I'll have a look at the list." He smiled at Ellie. "Are you two together?"

Ellie nodded. "My sister, Anna, doesn't drive so I brought her here."

Pastor Bob led them through the doorway and down the cool depths of a hallway, past a space labeled *Sanctuary,* to an austere room with a small window, a heavy oak desk, and two unmatched chairs. A simple wooden cross hung on the wall.

While the women tried to make themselves comfortable on the guest chairs, Pastor Bob slipped on reading glasses and typed in some commands on his keyboard. He studied the monitor. "When was your computer picked up, Mrs. Brewster?"

"December the twelfth," Iris answered. "I remember because I was going to a Christmas Open House in Beacon Hill, so I left the computer out on my porch that morning. The woman who answered the phone here had said that someone from the church would pick it up later that afternoon."

"Let's just have a look. What is your address?"

Iris gave it to him reluctantly, worried that her real name would show up.

"Hmm." He eyed Iris over his glasses. "It says that Iris Reid was the donor at that address."

Iris readjusted her phoney blond hair. "Oh, yes. She's our sister. Our other sister. She called to set up the donation, but it was my computer."

Pastor Bob frowned at the screen. "That's strange. There's a note here that says there was nothing on your porch to pick up when our volunteer came by at three that afternoon."

CHAPTER 17

Back in the Volvo, Iris glanced over her shoulder at the run-down facade of *the Church of the Little Lamb*. "Did those two strike you as criminal types?"

Ellie turned her key in the ignition. "Mousy Helen and dear Pastor Bob are as much criminals as my Aunt Betty and Uncle Jim from Indiana. I checked out the three rooms in the back and there were no stockpiles of computers or anything else. Pastor Bob saw me leaving the sanctuary, but I told him I had been in there praying, and thanked him for the opportunity."

Iris rubbed her hands in front of the dashboard vent that was beginning to crank out heat. "Do you have time to stop at the Deluxe Diner for some lunch? I'm starving and maybe we can figure this out while we eat."

Ellie gave her a thumbs up and headed into traffic.

"This thing itches." Iris slipped off the wig and threw it into her purse. She ran fingers through her liberated hair.

A mile further along Mount Auburn Street, Ellie swung into the parking lot of an authentic 1940's diner and they nabbed a newly-vacated booth inside the tiny space. A waitress, chewing a large wad of gum, swiped their table with a grimy rag and dealt out placemats and menus like playing cards.

Under the light from the aging halophane pendants, Iris' pot roast had a greenish cast but it tasted like buttery prime rib. Ellie pushed her turkey burger to one side and forked some pot roast onto her own plate.

When only a few crumbs remained, Ellie asked for coffee and Iris ordered a slice of warm cherry pie. "So, what do you make of Pastor Bob's claim that there was no computer to pick up on my porch? I distinctly remember putting it out on the Saturday before Christmas and I know it was gone when I returned from walking Sheba."

Ellie tipped cream from a tiny plastic container into her coffee. "Either someone stole the computer before the volunteer got there, or the volunteer picked it up to sell or hack into himself. Or we're really bad judges of character and Helen and Bob have just played us."

Iris took a sip of coffee. "Or maybe my bank information wasn't taken from the old computer after all. It could have come from one of those huge hacking break-ins at Target or T.J.Maxx. Or from god-knows-what other institution that's been violated. Nothing's safe anymore."

The fork stopped halfway to Ellie's lips. "In that case we'll never find out who's behind this."

CHAPTER 18

Iris spent the following week sending innumerable forms to credit agencies to try to repair the damage from the large balance on the credit card taken out in her name. All the while, she felt her doppelgänger gloating over the theft of not only her money but a big chunk of her pride.

Greg Peretti reported that no cash from the original bank robbery or any sign of the robbers themselves had surfaced yet. Iris' savings had been instantly vacuumed from Fidelity into an untraceable bank account in the Caymans. Peretti was still trying to track down the motorcycle.

Sterling assured her that the mounting evidence of identity theft should be enough to clear her from any involvement in the bank robbery and murder.

"Unless Lieutenant Choi can convince a jury that I've been planting that evidence."

So, while Iris kept looking over her shoulder, expecting the next disaster, she tried to turn her focus back to Luc's restaurant renovation.

She visited several of Milo Miller's previous projects. He

appeared to be a diamond-in-the-making. She especially liked the quality of the finish carpentry in a small jewelry store in Brookline. Birds-eye-maple cabinets, with tiny niches above, lined three walls of the shop. The owner, a stick-thin woman in her thirties named Gwen, wore an artsy and no-doubt-expensive tunic. She said that Milo had built all the cabinetry himself. "He's a complete perfectionist. I just wish I had another project for him. I loved being around his creative energy."

After Iris had talked to three more equally-effusive references and was assured that, perfectionism notwithstanding, Milo was able to bring jobs in on time and on budget, she arranged for Luc to meet this paragon at the site.

Luc would close on the property in two weeks' time, but the lawyers for the estate had given Iris access to the empty building so she could take measurements and document the work that needed to be done. She had already researched the code requirements for a restaurant kitchen, and Luc had outlined his own technical preferences for how he wanted things to be laid out.

*   *   *

The sun had finally returned on a Saturday morning in late March when Iris and Luc passed the last remaining clumps of dirty snow on Mass Ave as they headed to the site.

"Don't be put off by Milo's appearance," Iris warned. "He doesn't look like a contractor but, according to his references, he's very professional. And he does beautiful work."

As they approached the property's semi-circular driveway, Luc assured Iris, " If he knows his stuff, has a good team, and can work on a deadline, I'm good."

They were at the front door when they heard the rumble of a motorcycle. A helmeted figure in black leather, braid flying out behind, roared into the driveway.

"That's him?"

Iris nodded.

Milo dismounted and unfastened his helmet. He looked the three story Victorian house up and down, then walked toward them.

"Hi, Iris." Milo nodded at her then held out his hand to Luc. "Milo Miller. Looks like quite a project here."

Luc shook Milo's hand and led them inside.

Milo dug a notebook out of an inside pocket of his leather jacket and a tape measure from a zippered pocket. He looked around at the two large rooms on either side of the entry hall, then walked up close to a mantlepiece and inspected the woodwork. "Are you going to paint this?"

Iris looked at Luc, who shrugged. Then Iris said, "We'll decide that in the next two weeks. I'll have a full set of drawings and specifications for you then. We'll be fast-tracking the job to get it ready for an early September completion. That will work for your schedule, right?"

"Sure. I can gear up fast."

Luc led Milo around the house, describing what he would need in the kitchen, the cold room, the types of counters and prep sinks. Iris talked about the heating and electrical systems. They went down to the basement so Milo could see the existing equipment.

As they headed toward the mechanical room, Iris heard New Age music coming from one of the rooms in the finished section. She looked through a small window in a door and saw Hannah in a headstand surrounded by half a dozen women upended against the side walls.

Luc turned to Iris. "Did I tell you? Hannah doesn't have a problem renting this space while the upstairs is under construction."

CHAPTER 19

Rosica Bakalov waited outside a coffee house on Mass Ave, pretending to talk on her phone. Ever since Helen had called to warn her that a woman fitting the Reid woman's description had turned up at the church wanting her computer back, Rosica's mind had been in overdrive. She'd calmed Helen down, assuring the ninny that she would deal with Reid. Helen was definitely a weak link.

She'd been following Iris Reid for two days now, but the woman had stayed mostly inside, either in the big house on Washington Avenue or at the blond guy's place. Rosica was bundled up in her navy parka and jeans to blend in with the other Saturday morning errand-runners. She followed Reid and the blond guy who, she conceded, was good-looking but not her type, as they walked over to a ramshackle house with a For Sale sign. They'd waited a few minutes out front until a BMW motorcycle had roared up. The guy really needed to get his mufflers fixed. When the driver took off his helmet, Rosica had stood up straighter and shoved her phone into her pocket. *Be still, my heart. Who is that hot dude on the Beemer R-90S?* Now *he* was definitely Rosica's type, with that black braid and a hint of a tat on his neck. All three disappeared inside.

Mama still didn't know that Rosica had raided the woman's savings account. Maybe that *had* been taking the con too far. But who keeps almost a hundred K in a savings account? The mark was asking to be robbed. And now, based on Helen's information, the bitch was trying to turn the tables, to expose the Bakalov family's carefully-concealed tracks. That was not gonna happen. Rosica needed to get Iris Reid alone to issue a warning. Preferably without the damn dog.

CHAPTER 20

Back in the condo, Iris and Luc set about making lunch. Iris was becoming a salad specialist. She tossed multi-colored lettuces, nuts, seeds, and anything else "interesting" she could find into a bowl.

Luc had a white Bolognese sauce simmering on the cooktop, filling the kitchen with savory aromas. He lifted freshly made strands of tagliatelle ribbons from a drying rack with his hands and dropped the pasta into a saucepan of boiling water. "I don't want the space to look strictly Italian," he said, continuing a discussion they'd been having for several days. "I want it to be moody and elegant but without any particular country's stamp."

"Uh huh." Iris broke up some walnuts with her fingers and sprinkled them into the bowl. "I think we should use rich colors, but only ones from nature, the kind you can't really define as blue or green or gray because they change with the light. And adding some archways might make the transition between the rooms more fluid. The lighting could come from antique sconces on the surrounding walls for a warm, timeless look."

Luc closed his eyes. "Yeah, classic but still cool, not fussy."

He had designed the current Paradise Café himself with a

sort of Venice Beach, California vibe. Its light, airy room was painted pale taupe and had a long mahogany coffee bar that he had found in an antiques warehouse. The walls featured a rotating collection of paintings by local artists. At night, white tablecloths ratcheted up the formality, but the new restaurant would be more sophisticated still. Plus, it would only be open for dinner, not all day like the café. So, theoretically, Luc would have more spare time.

Iris set the wooden salad bowl down on the large pine table and tried to affect a casual tone. "Do you think it's a good idea to have a tenant in there during construction? What if Hannah or a student gets hurt stepping on a nail?"

"I didn't think of that." Luc joined her at the table and set down two bowls of pasta. "Maybe I should speak with her about safety precautions. She does walk around her studio with bare feet a lot."

Iris jabbed a perfectly al-dente noodle with her fork. *A lot? When had Luc seen Hannah in her studio? Maybe Iris should pay more attention to Yoga Girl.* "At the least, the noise of compressors and table saws won't make a very Zen background for her yoga classes."

"That shouldn't be a problem. Hannah says she can move her classes to the evenings or weekends when the work crew will be gone."

And Luc would be busy cooking then when the restaurant opens. She changed the subject. "We'll need to take out the front staircase so tipsy diners don't wander up into your living space. I measured the bar at the Café and it should fit perfectly in that space."

"Let's be sure to store all the staircase parts in the basement in case I ever need to put the building back together to sell it."

"Absolutely. All the Victorian carved woodwork makes it quite valuable. The back staircase off the kitchen is pretty tucked-away. We'll have to add a second egress stair somewhere." Iris gave Luc a long, thoughtful look. "Are you sure you want to get rid of your condo and live where you work?"

He speared a piece of baby lettuce. "I can't afford to keep the condo. I'll be pouring everything into the new restaurant. If it doesn't succeed, I don't know what I'll do."

Iris reached over and took his hand. "Are you kidding? This restaurant is going to blow Boston away."

CHAPTER 21

For Iris, the next week was a blur of long days split between designing at her drafting table and documenting on her computer all the work needed for the transformation.

Meanwhile, Luc was feverishly experimenting with new recipes in his condo's kitchen. Whenever Iris stopped work to drop by, she would get offered a wooden spoon filled with something delicious—mint-cucumber salsa, sautéed fiddlehead ferns, or poached rhubarb sauce, with Luc asking anxiously, "What do you think—honestly?"

Having her lover as a professional client was working out better than she'd expected. Luc liked her vision for the design. The few requests he made were for technical requirements for the kitchen. She was excited to have this degree of creative freedom and poured herself into producing a set of thirty drawings for Milo. From time to time, she thought wistfully about the Harvard project that had been snatched away from her so unfairly. She hoped that Vernon Elliott was flailing, out of his depth. Maybe this restaurant project would put her back on the architectural map.

On a Tuesday in early-April, around noon, Iris let herself

into Luc's condo with her key and found him standing at the kitchen island holding a glass of water and reading his mail. He was wearing nothing but bike shorts and his bare skin was glistening with perspiration. She gave herself a few seconds to appreciate the sight. "Hey, Cutie. It's forty degrees outside. Are you channeling August in here?"

Luc looked up and grinned. "I just took a hot yoga class. I can't believe how energized I feel. You have to try it."

"I thought these Yoga classes only met at night or on weekends."

"Hannah's going to switch the schedule after construction begins. She invited me to a semi-private class this morning to help me with my back problem. She's been really generous with her time."

CHAPTER 22

An hour later, Iris was still stewing over "generous Hannah" as she zipped along Storrow Drive. On her left, the Charles River glistened in the sun. *Maybe she could divert the Yogini's attention toward Milo. Surely the attractive contractor had a body part or two that needed special attention.*

She looped around onto Charles Street, the main artery of Beacon Hill, Boston's most historic neighborhood. Even though her destination was a half-dozen blocks away, she started her search for a parking spot. A block up she saw a woman standing on the sidewalk fishing for something in her purse. Iris aimed the Jeep at her like a heat seeking missile. Luckily, the woman pulled out her keys, not quarters, and pulled right out of the spot instead of spending the usual ten minutes talking on her phone.

Iris had dropped the "bid set" drawings off with Milo that morning so he could prepare a fixed cost proposal for Luc, but their fast-track schedule allowed her no down time. She'd specified allowances for certain fixtures and built-ins. Now she needed to start stockpiling the items on her list. It was never easy to find what she wanted, when she wanted it. And because she was planning to secure fixtures with a one-of-a-kind look, the process would be that much more time-consuming.

It had been a while since she'd been to Beacon Hill, and she ambled along the brick Charles Street sidewalks, looking in the store front windows as she passed. The neighborhood had a small-scale village atmosphere with nary a chain store in sight. The Beacon Hill Historic Commission went to extraordinary lengths to keep all twenty-first century intrusions at bay. Which made the loud growl of a motorcycle seem incongruous as a driver revved its motor at a newly-green traffic light.

Iris turned right on Chestnut Street and saw the antiques store on the next corner. She was relieved to see the discrete "open" sign hanging from the door knob as belatedly she remembered that Rupert's schedule was less than orthodox and she'd forgotten to call ahead. When she entered the shop, filled cheek-by-jowl with furniture, a chubby bulldog trotted over to sniff her feet.

From a chair behind a large Regency desk, a broad-shouldered black man looked up from his laptop. His face lit up and he rose. "Iris, it's been a donkey's age. How *are* you?"

They exchanged double kisses and spent a few minutes catching up on each other's lives. Iris told Rupert about Luc's new restaurant and the pieces she was looking for. He raised a finger, stood, and took her by the arm into the shop's second room. "You need to see these delicious repro sconces. I have a workshop near

Torino that's been making them for me, and we can fabricate any quantity you want."

When Iris saw what Rupert was pointing at, she couldn't help but smile. Bronze hands reached out of the wall to hold torches with lampshades on them. "Perfect! Just the right amount of whimsy. I can't believe they're not antiques." She peered at them and admired the workmanship. Then, taking out her phone, she photographed the fixtures from all sides and wrote down their measurements. She and Rupert negotiated a price for a dozen of them and Iris said she'd call to confirm the order after showing the photos to Luc.

As she and Rupert were talking, a movement caught her eye. A slight figure in a black sweatshirt with the hood covering half the face was talking on a phone across the street. Iris couldn't tell if it was a male or female, but she could see a red and yellow mark on the person's wrist. She and the caller locked eyes for a split second and she heard a tiny warning go off like a dog whistle that only she could hear. The figure jogged out of sight before Iris could finish up with Rupert, and by the time she exited the shop, she'd forgotten all about it.

Iris failed to notice the person, now with the hoodie rolled up in a backpack and holding a motorcycle helmet, following her down the sidewalk from a block away.

CHAPTER 23

Iris wedged her Jeep into the fast-flowing, bumper-to-bumper stream of white-knuckled drivers on Route 93, a highway that was sunk under Boston's streets and skyscrapers. She drove south for twenty minutes before peeling off at the Dorchester exit and pulling into the dirt parking lot of a low-slung warehouse.

She needed to find a focal piece for the right-side dining room that would balance the impressive fireplace in the left-side room. While she wasn't sure exactly what she needed, she did know where to look. Beantown Salvage was a venerable architectural salvage yard filled with over-sized antique treasures and discards.

The interior hadn't changed in the five years since she'd been there last. As usual, the store seemed deserted. Iris wandered down aisle after aisle of perilously-stacked artifacts. Old doors in varying states of disrepair were lined up in a dozen rows, labeled by size. Elaborate mantlepieces, with and without carved over-mantles, were shoved up against the wall in another section. Windows, some stained-glass, others with tiny mullioned panes, had their own turf. When she paused to rummage through a barrel of glass doorknobs, she almost knocked over a large Victorian newel post but caught it just in time.

She thought she heard faint footsteps several aisles away. *Great, maybe it's a salesperson and I won't have to trudge all the way back to the office for help if I find anything I like.*

She continued wandering until she found the section she was looking for. Huge bookshelves, dark-wood hutches, and other oversized cabinetry which had been ripped out of Victorian houses and were no longer fashionable for the twenty-first century stood abandoned in a dusty corner.

Iris examined a dozen different chests and cabinets before she narrowed her choices down to two pieces that looked promising. She took a tape measure and notebook out of her purse to jot down their details. One was a breakfront, eight feet tall by eight feet wide, with glass doors on the upper section and solid cabinets below. The section in the middle part stepped out. Delicate lines of lead traced out a pattern of flowers, which she realized were irises, in the glass. Perfect. It could be her secret signature on the project, unrecognized by most of the patrons.

With a half smile she turned to study the second piece, a cabinet even more massive than the breakfront. It was interesting, an ornately carved mahogany box with arched glass doors. But Iris wondered if it looked a little too "decoratory". She stood back a foot and held up her hands to block the view of the sides. The glass doors themselves were quite elegant. Maybe Milo could build a new, simpler mahogany box with shelves inside and just use the doors from this white elephant to create something new, but with an aged patina, to hold the restaurant's stemware and plates.

Iris would have to check the price to see if it was worth paying for the whole thing just to use the doors, but her first choice was the breakfront. She'd photograph both pieces to text to Luc before hunting down a salesperson.

Just as Iris backed up to get a good camera angle, she heard an ominous creaking sound. Instinctively she dove to one side, landing on the floor seconds before the breakfront crashed down to land where she'd been standing. The sound reverberated throughout the warehouse and splintered glass flew everywhere. She ducked her head under her arms, her heart thudding, her hands scraped raw from cushioning her fall.

After a moment, she looked up to see a man with a gray halo of wispy hair staring down at her.

"You all right?"

"No!" Iris picked slivers of glass out of her hair. "What happened? How did this thing tip over?"

The concern on his face turned to wariness. "You must have bumped into it."

"I didn't touch it."

"Are you sure you didn't move it around?" He scratched the

back of his head as he regarded the wooden carcass and shards of glass at his feet. "This was an expensive piece and now it's kindling."

"How could I have pushed it from behind? I was in front of it." Iris gingerly picked her way through the rubble to where the breakfront had been standing. The old wood floor looked level enough and it didn't appear as if anything heavy had been leaning against the piece. She studied the walls and ceiling. "Do you have any security cameras in here? Maybe we can see what caused the crash."

"Yeah, in the office. I was watching the ball-game which is why I didn't notice you come in."

Iris' face stung. She patted it as she followed the man back through the labyrinth to his cubbyhole of an office. She noticed blood on her hand.

The man introduced himself as Carl. He checked three monitors on his desk to identify the one showing the furniture section. As he rewound the tape, they watched as a shadow passed across a corner of the screen in reverse motion.

"Look! There *was* someone else here. Play it forward," Iris practically shouted.

"Well, I'll be damned," Carl muttered and froze the image as he got to the right frame.

Iris could make out herself and the breakfront but saw only

the back of a blurry figure in the area behind the big cabinets. The angle made it impossible to see the person's hands and the resolution was too grainy to tell much about what the person looked like.

"Lots of people look at the furniture. Doesn't look to me like this guy pushed it over."

"Well *I* didn't touch it," Iris protested, "So, either this guy pushed it or it was unstable to begin with."

Carl cleared his throat. "Let's check the other tapes to see if we can get a better shot of him."

They saw nothing on the second screen and only a blurry shadow entering quickly through the front door on the first one. Oddly enough, backing that tape up didn't show anyone exiting through that door after the crash.

"I guess I can get insurance to cover it," Carl muttered.

"Do you have any cameras out in the parking lot?"

"No, why would we need to see out there?"

"Hang on—" Iris ran outside. She saw only her Jeep and a truck with the Beantown Salvage logo on the side.

Iris pulled out her phone and punched in Sterling's number. She explained what had happened.

"Time to call in the police," he said.

CHAPTER 24

Iris had vowed she'd never spend another minute inside Cambridge police headquarters and yet here she sat in the same interview room where she'd been questioned months ago before she'd ended up in a holding cell. Sterling hadn't been able to break away from a deposition to join her. Beads of dampness formed in her armpits.

Lieutenant Choi had her repeat the events that occurred at Beantown Salvage and the not-terribly-helpful description of the person who she believed was watching her at Rupert's Antique Store on Beacon Hill.

While Iris signed her statement, Choi took a phone call. She wandered over to the door and turned her back to Iris. "You sure it was recent? Uh, huh. The CSIs got a decent cast of it? Can they tell what kind of motorcycle?" Choi turned toward Iris and noticed her look of keen curiosity. Choi lowered her voice. "Send me the report."

When Iris finally left the building on Sixth Street, she took several deep breaths of fresh air and sent a text to Ellie.

It was five p.m. when Iris and Ellie entered the Paradise Café.

It was almost empty. Louise, the waitress with the nose ring, was getting the unoccupied tables ready for the dinner crowd. When she looked up and saw Iris, she headed straight for the kitchen.

Iris could imagine what she must look like with her new facial cuts from the exploding glass. She sank into a chair and tried discretely to sniff her armpits. The adrenaline spike from earlier had left her system and sapped her energy.

Luc swung through the kitchen door, wiping his hands on his apron, and hurried over to Iris. "Are you all right? What happened?"

Ellie answered, "An enormous breakfront fell on top of her at the building salvage place."

Luc sat down and took Iris' hand. "Oh, God, tell me everything. What's a breakfront?"

After Iris filled him in on her afternoon, Ellie carefully picked a sliver of glass out of Iris' hair. "Lucky you have cat-like reflexes," Ellie said.

Luc shook his head. "A guy knocks over a big piece of furniture on you and doesn't even stop to see if you're OK?"

"I'm not absolutely sure he pushed it. He might have bumped against it accidentally or he might not have known I was there. He probably ran out because he didn't want to pay for the damage."

Ellie gave Iris a sympathetic nod. "I've been in Beantown

Salvage and that place is a mine field. Everything's stacked up just waiting to fall over."

Iris found two aspirins in her purse and dry-swallowed them. "Lieutenant Choi is looking into it. Maybe she can enhance the tapes to see what actually happened. I'm fine now."

Arnold, Luc's sous-chef, poked his head out the kitchen door. "Chef, do you want me to season the bouillabaisse?"

Luc stood up, then looked back at Iris. "Are you sure you're OK?"

She nodded and he leaned down to kiss her. "I'll swing by after work. We can talk about this some more. Maybe you need my bodyguard services."

After he retreated to the kitchen, Ellie gave Iris a long, appraising look. "You think it was deliberate, don't you?"

Iris massaged a tender spot at the nape of her neck. "I have been wondering if the person behind me in the salvage place could be the same person that I noticed outside the antiques store in Beacon Hill. And that person might be a 'she' not a 'he'."

"You think your doppelgänger's stalking you now?"

"Doesn't it seem like too many things are happening for them to be coincidences?"

CHAPTER 25

Iris spent Sunday morning in bed with Luc and all thoughts of her scare at Beantown Salvage faded into memory. The two eventually migrated to her kitchen window seat and, while Iris pored over the Sunday *Globe,* thankfully free of any mention of herself or the bank robbery, Luc whipped up some Huevos Rancheros for brunch.

At around one, Luc left to watch the Red Sox game at his sister's house, so Iris decided to spend an hour or two working on the restaurant project. Normally, she tried to keep her weekends work-free but, with this crazy fast-track schedule, she wasn't going to have a full day off until she'd pinned down some technical details and sourced all of the owner-supplied materials.

Ninety minutes later she knew more about grease scrubbers for restaurant vent hoods than she'd ever wanted to know. She could also reel off all the dimensions required for a unisex, handicap-accessible bathroom.

She stood up from the computer, stretched her arms, and caught Sheba giving her a purposeful stare.

"Sorry, Shebz. You'll have to make do with a quick walk to Raymond Park today. I have karate at four."

Iris stuffed a tennis ball in her jacket pocket and they trotted along Upland Road to the park. Gradually, as they drew nearer, the hairs on the back of Iris' neck began to prickle. She had the distinct feeling that she was being watched. She peered around at everyone on the sidewalks, but no one looked suspicious. In the fenced-in park, Iris threw the ball for Sheba until the dog's energy wound down. Afterward, she hurried Sheba back to the house.

Iris decided to drive to the dojo, even though it was an easy ten minute walk. She didn't like the idea that her doppelgänger might be watching her. And if she was, Iris wanted to make sure that her reflexes were in peak readiness. Maybe she should go to the dojo more often. Her martial arts skills had helped her fend off a vicious attacker just the previous year.

She changed into a *gi* in the locker room, carefully wrapping and tying her brown belt around her waist. Bowing first before the portrait of Grand Master Uechi, she entered the dojo and joined the other brown belts kneeling before their instructor, Sensei Ono, before beginning the class.

Her karate skills would not protect her from an opponent with a gun, or even a knife. Her branch of karate specialized in close-in fighting, getting your opponent off-balance or using his momentum against him. Once mastered, those techniques would allow her to outmaneuver someone stronger than herself.

Karate is fifty percent mental and fifty percent physical. Iris tried to clear her mind of fear and to focus on her breathing as the class performed *katas*—the ritualized animal movements that they used as warm-ups, then conditioning drills. Iris paired off for sparring with a tall woman who easily had forty pounds on her. They strapped on red hand and head protectors, then bowed to each other before beginning to grapple.

Iris focused on precision as they stepped through a ballet of moves—attacking and escaping, blocking and counter-attacking, all the while controlling her punches so that they merely tapped her opponent's vulnerable spots.

By the end of class, Iris' skin was coated with sweat. She bowed again to her partner and headed back to the locker room. She felt alive, and she intended to stay that way.

CHAPTER 26

Rosica cursed in Bulgarian the whole way back from Beantown Salvage. Who knew a woman Iris Reid's age could have such quick reflexes? Rosica would have to be smarter next time. Now, as she propped her motorcycle up onto its center stand in the East Cambridge driveway, she had to admit that she'd relied too much on improvisation. Her instincts had served her well in the past, but this new adversary was tougher than she had expected. She'd have to think out her strategies.

She tossed her helmet onto the sofa as she headed upstairs to check on Mama, half hoping the old woman would pick a fight so Rosica could let off some steam. Twenty minutes later, still grouchy, she returned to the kitchen to make herself a rum and Diet Coke cocktail. She deposited herself at the small Formica table by the window. The faded beige wallpaper with those stupid clusters of wheat, left from the previous owners, depressed her. It made her feel like she lived in an old person's house. She *did* live in an old person's house.

Just how much had the Reid woman been able to piece together about their operation? The police would have told her that someone had gotten a driver's license and credit card in Reid's name. She probably knew that her savings account had been raided as well. But how had she made the connection to her old donated computer? Rosica had counted on being far away by the time that link was discovered. She had no intention of spending any time in this new country behind bars. Still, Helen said that Reid seemed to be fishing, so maybe the woman still hadn't realized that she was on the right track.

Rosica slid a pack of Lucky Strikes out of her shirt pocket, tapped one out, and propped it into the corner of her mouth, flicking a spark on her plastic lighter. She sucked in a deep hit of nicotine. *What else did the bitch know?*

The day before, Rosica had hidden in the bushes of the big house on Washington Avenue to peek in the windows. She'd noted that Reid didn't have to live in a house with her invalid mother and idiot brothers. She got to fix up her own house as she chose, probably going to a high-end store to buy any furniture she wanted. She probably paid other people to paint the walls whatever color she fancied, never mind keeping old wallpaper. If Iris Reid changed her mind, she'd get them to paint it another color. Why not? Rosica leaned back in her chair and blew out a smoke ring.

A woman like that got her pick of men, too. The blond one followed her like a puppy dog. He probably never hit her, even when he got drunk. And the hot guy with the motorcycle—Reid seemed to be in charge of him too. He'd been listening to her, nodding his head. She was probably sleeping with both of them. *American women—no morals!*

Rosica was glad she'd stolen the Reid woman's money. It was her turn for a chance at the good life in America. She drained her cocktail and noticed an edge of the dreadful wallpaper starting to peel near the refrigerator. She walked over and started to strip it away from the wall. A large sheet came off easily. She dug her fingers under an adjacent piece and pulled.

CHAPTER 27

Iris rummaged through the refrigerator to find some tasty leftover scraps for Sheba as the dog sat at her feet, following her every move. Iris could feel heat radiating off her skin after her sparring session. She had held her own against a much larger opponent, which reassured her after the unsettled feeling of being followed at the park that afternoon.

She found some bits of last night's chicken, mixed them into Sheba's kibble, and set down the dog's bowl, then poured herself a glass of Grüner Vetliner, and headed to her favorite window seat. Outside, dusk was settling in and the darkened trees, outlined by a lighter gray sky, bent and swayed. She checked her cell phone for messages, found nothing of interest, then texted Luc: *Dinner here? My turn to cook.* She got a quick response: *You're on. See you in a half hour.*

Iris changed into a pretty flowered dress that Luc had given her for her birthday the week before. It was a little lightweight for mid April so she'd added a cashmere cardigan. Back in the kitchen, she started sifting through the photos on her phone. She wanted to show Luc the arched mahogany and glass doors from the salvage place since the breakfront was no longer an option. As she scrolled through her photos from the warehouse, she looked for any suggestive shadows but found none. It had been dark inside. She'd taken only a blurry shot of the mahogany piece before she'd had to hit the floor. But Luc should be able to get the idea of it, and she could bring him back to the warehouse to see it in person if he wanted.

She kept scrolling. The photos of the wall sconces from Rupert's shop were much clearer. The workmanship on the brass hands was of a high quality. She hoped that Luc wouldn't consider the fixtures overly playful. She grinned at the next photo which showed Rupert's chubby bulldog drooling in the bottom of the frame. What caught Iris' eye next was a large mirror mounted on the wall next to the sconce. An image of the street was reflected in it. The figure in the black hoodie stood staring into the shop.

Iris went through the rest of her photos to see if there were any other sightings of this person, but this was the only one. She e-mailed the shot to her computer, then moved to her home office and swung her chair around to face her monitor. She dragged the pdf from her mailbox into a photoshop program file. Tucking her lip under her teeth in concentration, she enlarged and cropped the image, then peered in close to study the frame. She did some more editing of the brightness and sharpened the clarity.

Iris hadn't been wrong—there was a small tattoo visible on

the inside of the person's thin wrist which held a cell phone up to the side of the hoodie. The tattoo looked like a yellow creature of some sort on a red background. Besides that, she could make out a backpack and something the person was holding in the other hand. The object was a large white dome with light reflecting off it. A motorcycle helmet.

Although the hood of the sweatshirt covered half of the person's face, Iris could see one exposed eye with long dark eyelashes. It was a woman.

CHAPTER 28

By the time Luc let himself in through Iris' kitchen door, she had whipped together a salad and quickly emptied a bag of Trader Joe's frozen mushroom risotto into a frying pan with a little water. She'd covered the pan of simmering rice and hidden the incriminating bag at the bottom of the garbage container.

Luc came over to the stove and nuzzled the back of her neck. "Nice dress. Something smells good." He lifted the lid and laughed, "Cooking all afternoon I see."

Iris grabbed the lid from him. "You said you liked this risotto."

He kissed her neck and said, "I love this risotto."

She gave him a playful push. "Make yourself useful, Cormier, and pour us some wine while I cook the salmon." Iris stirred the risotto and unwrapped the fish. "I have something to show you."

"Good—I need something to distract me from the drubbing the Red Sox took today." Luc found the chilled bottle of white wine in the refrigerator, filled two glasses, and carried them over to the table.

After setting the skillet over a medium flame, Iris went to the printer in her office next to the kitchen to pick up the cropped photo enlargement showing the woman in the hoodie. She placed it in front of Luc, with a magnifying glass, before slipping into her seat and taking a large sip of wine.

"Who's this?" Luc asked.

"She was watching me when I was in Rupert's shop yesterday." Iris bit at the cuticle on her thumb. "She has a motorcycle helmet there—see? And the police found recent motorcycle tracks in the Beantown Salvage parking lot."

Luc looked up sharply. "You think this is her? That she followed you and pushed over that chest-thing to try to kill you?"

"A woman in her early twenties, who rides a motorcycle, stole my identity, robbed a bank and implicated me, then cleaned out my savings account? Is it such a stretch to believe she's stalking me now and trying to kill me?"

A timer went off and Iris got up to flip the fish.

"Who is this bitch and what does she have against you?"

"I wish I knew. I didn't think anyone hated me enough to want me dead."

She returned to the table and looked over Luc's shoulder as he studied the photo through the magnifying glass.

"What's the tatt on her wrist?" he asked. "Maybe we can identify her through that."

"Mmmm...a dog? What do you think?"

"Yeah, could be a fuzzy yellow dog. Maybe a gang emblem. That might narrow things down."

"I wish I could get the resolution better." Iris headed back to the stove, spooned the fish and rice onto plates, then set them at their places.

Luc raised his eyes to her. "You know who could do that—the cops. And if you're right about this woman following you and trying to kill you, you need to show them this picture so they can protect you."

"They're not taking me seriously. I told Lieutenant Choi about this person yesterday and she didn't seem to think that the incident at the salvage place was anything but an accident."

"But now you have a picture showing that the person you thought was following you is a young woman, probably the same one who impersonated you at the bank robbery. It's hard to see what she looks like, but it might be enough if they've arrested her before. Especially if her tatt sets off any bells."

Iris pushed up the sleeves of her sweater and rubbed her arms. "You think so? Maybe I'll call Choi tomorrow."

"Let me go with you. You shouldn't be alone with this maniac on the loose."

Iris was about to say something, but changed her mind. "Thanks."

CHAPTER 29

Iris spent a sleepless night worrying about when and where another attack might take place. The frantic hamster wheel in her head kept producing new possibilities. Seeing that woman's face made the previously vague menace real.

She called Lieutenant Choi the next morning. Choi told her to e-mail the photo right away, then meet her at police headquarters at ten.

Luc had left Iris' bed at the ungodly hour of five-thirty to go to the wholesale market to stock up on supplies for the day. He'd be at the Café by now, writing up the menu for tonight's dinner. She texted him about the ten o'clock appointment.

*   *   *

An hour later, Iris and Luc were escorted to a small office on the third floor of Cambridge Police headquarters with a sign next to the door: Audio-Visual Services. The heat was on way too high in the windowless room and Donna Choi was down to her shirtsleeves. She hovered over a small man with bloodshot eyes, and the two of them looked up briefly from what they were studying on his computer monitor.

Choi motioned them in, belatedly seeming to notice that there were no extra seats. "We can stand. This shouldn't take long. Stan here has taken the jpeg you sent me as far as he can."

Iris and Luc moved around to study the image on the screen. The resolution was slightly sharper, but it was still difficult to see what the woman looked like.

Stan zoomed in on the tattoo. As Iris leaned in for a closer look, she noticed a ripe smell. The plastic cover of a bologna sandwich lay partially unwrapped on the desk nearby. She leaned away quickly.

"Is it a lion... or maybe a dragon?" Iris asked. "And what's that red blob behind it? "

"That's what we were trying to figure out when you arrived," Lieutenant Choi said. "It may be a crime family's crest from the old country. The red may be a shield. You don't recognize it?"

"Why should *I* recognize it?"

Lieutenant Choi and Stan exchanged looks, then she said, "You're telling me this woman has been stalking you and tried to kill you but you have no idea who she is?

"That's right—I have no idea who she is or why she's doing this. It started with the bank robbery when she pretended to be me. Now it keeps escalating."

Luc held up his hand palm-out. "Iris needs protection. This woman almost killed her. What are you waiting for?"

"For one thing, Mr. Cormier, we don't know who this woman is and we have no evidence that ties her to Ms. Reid. Our job is to enforce the law, not to arrest people for standing on the sidewalk talking on their phone."

Iris swallowed. "So the tattoo is the best lead you have?"

"And it's a promising lead. Stan will run the image through our tattoo recognition database. That's our best bet. I doubt that the facial recognition software will get a hit from this partial view. But if we can track down the tattoo, maybe we can figure out some connection between her and Ms. Reid."

Iris didn't like the way Lieutenant Choi lumped her together with her stalker as if they were partners-in-crime.

CHAPTER 30

Back at the house on Washington Avenue, Luc helped Iris measure all of the first floor windows. Afterward, they returned to Luc's condo with Iris' packed suitcase and Sheba. Iris called up Insta-shade on her I-pad and started filling out an order form while Luc made lunch.

"I can't believe I have to turn my house into a fortress because of this person," Iris complained from the kitchen table.

Luc stopped pouring some chilled lemon soup and gently rested the glass container on the island counter next to a pair of bowls. There were a few moments of silence before he said, "Why don't you hold off on placing that order. I have a better idea. Move in here with me."

Without looking up from her I-pad, Iris said, "I thought I just did. You must be getting sick of me camping out here."

Hearing no response, she glanced up and noticed Luc's serious expression. "Wait—did you mean *really* move in?"

Luc poured soup into the bowls. "I know this place is too small for you to have a real office here, but the new property will have lots more space."

She regarded him, pleasure at his willingness to take this step warring with her horror at the idea of losing the home she'd inherited from her parents. Sensing Luc's vulnerability, something inside her gave a little and she rose to her feet.

"You could design our upstairs living space anyway you want," he said.

She wrapped her arms around his waist and kissed him.

Sheba waddled over and sat at their feet, panting and blinking up at them.

Luc held her away from him and studied her face. "You look worried. I know I work crazy hours, but I can have Allegra take more nights after the new restaurant gets going."

Iris shook her head. "No, no, I'd love to live with you. It's just that... my house has a lot of memories and..." She trailed off.

He held her gaze.

"But we can figure out the logistics," she assured him. "Meanwhile, we can set ourselves up together here and I can go back to work at the Washington Avenue house if I need to."

CHAPTER 31

"Why are we meeting here?" Ellie looked around the narrow railroad car of space in Simon's coffeehouse, a block from Luc's condo. "Isn't this one of Luc's competitors?"

"Not for long," Iris said. "Luc's getting out of the coffeeshop end of the business so you and I will need to find a new hang-out." Iris leaned on the glass counter to put in both of their decaf orders. "Besides, I want to stick to public places where my nemesis can't creep up on me. And I have some news for you, but I didn't want to tell you in front of Luc."

"Good news or bad news?"

Iris scanned the dozen lined-up tables looking for an empty one. "Jeez. It's two in the afternoon and this place is packed."

A young man rose to leave, bussing his dirty cup, and Ellie swooped into an empty seat at the vacated table. She repeated to Iris "Good or bad?"

"Good, but complicated."

The barista called out their names, and Iris returned a moment later from the counter with two giant cups. "I put one sugar in yours."

"No more stalling. Spill."

"Luc asked me to move in with him."

Ellie took a careful sip. "As in, all the time?"

Iris sighed. "As in sell my house and move into the apartment above the new restaurant."

"You can't get rid of your house. Your parents lived there! And now you've finally fixed it up the way you like it."

"Luc says that I can do that with the new place."

Ellie pursed her lips as if she were trying to figure out how to say something diplomatically. "Are you sure you're ready for this?"

Her friend knew Iris' pathetic history with men. Iris worked with clients, carpenters, plumbers and electricians, no problem. But when it came to men she dated, she'd left behind a string of disasters, including her brief marriage. For a long time before Luc, she'd spent most of her free time alone.

"Good question." Iris started to break up a wooden stir-stick. "I love Luc, and when I saw how open he was making himself...I couldn't say no. Relationships are like sharks. They have to keep moving forward or they die."

"Actually, I heard on NPR that that's not technically true."

Iris shot her a look.

"Luc's divorce just came through two or three months ago." Ellie drained her coffee. "Do you think *he's* ready for this?"

"He was separated from his wife for a year before that. And this was his idea."

"I guess you can always rent out your house in case things don't work out," Ellie pointed out.

"You're such a romantic." By then, a small pile of shredded stirrer sticks stood next to Iris' cup.

CHAPTER 32

Not even her best friend, Ellie, knew why the thought of letting go of the Queen Anne house with its distinctive turret left Iris feeling so bereft.

She stared out Luc's kitchen window. Sterling had inherited their father's Roman nose and Iris had gotten their mother's thick chestnut hair and fine features, but it had been the bequest of this house to Iris and her brother that had made the strongest impact. It hadn't been her childhood home. The Reids had moved to Cambridge for John Reid's teaching post at Harvard while Iris was starting college a full state away at Dartmouth. Only when she decided to go to architecture school at the Harvard GSD did she spend any time in the house for the brief year and a half before her parents were killed on an icy New Hampshire highway.

She already had painful memories of her parents long before their car crashed into a tree. During her Junior year in high school, Iris had paid an unannounced visit to her father's office. She'd discovered her cold, remote father embracing his teaching assistant. Passionately embracing. A total cliché. Her father's eyes had met hers before Iris could flee but, in the deeply repressed style of their family, they'd never discussed the incident. And, maybe because of that, his duplicity had become radioactive in her mind. Her own silence, meant to protect her mother, came to feel like complicity. Throughout Iris' remaining time in high school, she'd tried to avoid thinking about her father's frequent late nights at "work" and her mother's tight-lipped air of stoic resignation.

By the time her parents moved to Cambridge, Iris felt relieved to see them go. She'd avoided going home during college breaks and spent her summers working various jobs up in Hanover. Later, while attending architecture school in Cambridge, she began to make some efforts to bridge the divide between herself and her parents. She began talking with her mother more, although they never came close to confronting the reality of her father's affair. By the time the sympathetic police officer had showed up at her desk at graduate school to tell her about her parents' accident, Iris had come to feel closer to Vera Reid than she'd ever felt before.

Weeks after, huddled next to Sterling on an uncomfortable leather settee, across from the estate lawyer's imposing desk, Iris had felt numb. That feeling turned into confusion when the lawyer had explained the odd provisions of their parents' will. In the case of their mother dying first, the entire estate would have gone to the Hood Museum at Dartmouth where her father had taught art history for most of his career. But in the case of their father dying first, the estate would go to their mother, with a codicil that it would get passed to their two children after her death.

As it happened, her father had died instantly after the crash. A truck driver had stopped at the accident scene and later attested to the fact that Vera Reid was still breathing when he'd found her in the mangled passenger's seat—barely breathing, but still alive. It was due to their mother's final agonizing minutes that Iris and Sterling inherited the house and their modest savings.

It had taken Iris a good long while to sort out her feelings about all this. At first, she had viewed the house as a tainted thing. She hated her father for the way he had treated the family while alive, and for his final *screw you* will and testament message which underscored his real priorities.

After graduate school, Iris had fled south to New York City to start a new life. During her time there, and with the help of a good therapist, she'd found a different way of viewing these two people who had been responsible for her creation. She saw that her mother's love had always been there. Even if Vera Reid had never been able to stand up to her husband, she'd found her own ways to circumvent his selfishness.

Almost suddenly, after three years' work, it became important to Iris to live in the house that her mother had so fastidiously left behind for her and her brother. She moved back to Cambridge and, with her proceeds from their life insurance, bought out Sterling's share of the house.

She'd had no hesitation selling off its fusty antique furniture, little by little replacing it with the Modernist pieces she preferred. Fifteen years later, having made the house completely her own, she felt that she'd finally performed a long-overdue exorcism.

Iris absently fiddled with the stem of the oversized, black-faced Movado watch on her left wrist. It was the same one the police had returned to her with the rest of her father's personal effects after the accident. She wasn't really sure why she still wore it. She just knew that it was related to a certain emptiness inside her. Maybe someday she could fill it.

CHAPTER 33

On Monday afternoon, Rosica sat in the Mass Ave Starbucks staring at her laptop. She looked up nervously. This wasn't one of Iris Reid's hang-outs, but you never knew. She had finally tracked down the dress, the long flowered dress that Reid had been wearing the night before when Rosica had watched through the window as Reid and the blond guy ate dinner. One hundred and sixty-five dollars! Who paid that much money for a dress to wear when you weren't even going out to a restaurant? Reid had worn it with a soft-looking sweater and boots and, Rosica had to admit, she'd looked classy.

Rosica sat back and crossed her arms. At one point she'd thought that the blond guy had spotted her, but then his attention went to something Reid was showing him on a piece of paper. Rosica had slowly sunk down into the bushes, getting scratched in the process, and high-tailed it out of there. It was stupid to keep taking these chances.

She sipped her black coffee and looked over at the barista who had smiled at her so warmly ten minutes before. He was leaning over the counter chatting with another woman.

Iris Reid didn't know where she was living and probably couldn't recognize her the way she looked now with short blond hair and punk clothes. As long as Rosica stopped doing stupid things like peering in windows, she was invisible. Even if Reid had made the connection between a fake credit card and her old computer, she still wouldn't be able to track the ID theft to her. Rosica knew how to cover her tracks.

She'd jumped to conclusions thinking Reid was on her trail and needed to be eliminated. *That* could have left a trail. Way too risky. Luckily she'd found an open window and gotten away from the furniture warehouse clean, and there hadn't been an opportunity at the dog park for Rosica to make a move. What was it the street girls used to say? *No harm, no foul.*

Rosica idly scrolled through the information about the dress. The material was viscose, whatever that was. She pinch-zoomed on the flower print, then bookmarked the page and closed the laptop.

After finishing her last swallow of her coffee, she sat up straight and stretched her neck to either side. Actually, she was the lucky one, not Iris Reid. Rosica and her brothers had pulled off a successful robbery, paid off Mama's mortgage, and she'd even created her own secret stash thanks to Reid's generous savings account.

She reopened her laptop, went to the shopping page, and clicked 'buy now'.

CHAPTER 34

The day had finally come. The new-bloom scent of early May floated in the air. Mud season had turned into that glorious but short-lived period known as Spring in New England. It was time to "break ground" for the new project, though this job didn't require any exterior work, so no ground was actually being "broken." Luc, as the owner, wasn't going to stand in the front yard in a hard hat nudging a shovel into the earth with his well-shod, Italian-booted foot.

Instead, a sleepy Iris arrived at the site just after eight a.m. and noted with approval the official orange building permit displayed in a front window. She pushed open the heavy front door and was immediately engulfed in a cloud of plaster dust. Through the white haze she could see several masked workers dismantling the front staircase to the second floor. The demolition crew resembled the local chapter of Hell's Angels. Loud heavy metal rock poured out of an unseen radio.

Iris held a hand over her mouth and approached the closest demo guy, a short heavily-muscled man in a torn black *Miller Construction* T-shirt wielding a crowbar. On closer inspection, she saw he was prying a handrail from the wall with considerable care, almost surgically. He handed her a paper mask.

"Thanks. Is Milo here?" she shouted over the roar of an air compressor.

"Back there." The man tipped his head to the building's rear.

Iris found Milo in the kitchen marking up blueprints. He was still wearing leather pants, a look Iris found impractical for a construction site but intriguingly flattering. Was he even going to wear them on muggy days in July?

He looked up. "Hey."

She returned his "hey" and bent over the drawings to see what he was doing.

He handed her a print-out of a bar chart. "This is the schedule I'll need to follow if we're going to get Luc in here by September. I marked the dates when I'll need certain fixtures and other owner-supplied materials on site. Let me know if you see any problem, OK?"

Milo had methodically scribbled notes on the floor plans about vendors for him to call for various construction materials.

Iris was impressed by his organization. She had worked with her share of seat-of-their-pants contractors. "Are you going to be on site every day?"

"Planning to," he answered. "How 'bout you?"

"Uh, huh." Today was the ritual sizing-up when architect and contractor tried to take the measure of each other's working style. Iris liked what she saw so far.

"When do you think you'll demo upstairs?" she asked.

"The guys will take out these kitchen cabinets next. I'm having Boston Resources pick them up for recycling. Then we'll move upstairs this afternoon to demo the walls and take the bathrooms down to the studs." Milo paused and cleared his throat. "Is that woman going to keep giving yoga classes in the basement? I'm nervous about my insurance if any of her students step on a nail or something."

"Luc told Hannah that she had to have her students use the basement entrance. And the classes are switching to evenings and weekends soon. They won't be coming through here."

"Good." Milo nodded and went back to writing his notes.

Iris retreated to a door in the hall and headed up the smaller staircase to the second floor, the part of the building that would be her new home. She and Luc would have to leave this door locked during the evenings so that no confused restaurant patrons would invade their space while looking for a restroom. This was one of the aspects of moving in upstairs that made Iris uneasy. Another was that she'd have to escort her dog down a flight of stairs and wait around while Sheba took care of business in the small back yard.

At the head of the stairs, Iris looked down a long hallway.

This level was divided up into five bedrooms and two bathrooms. Iris had redesigned the space to accommodate two bedrooms and her office along with a kitchen, dining room and living room. With an addition of two bathrooms, it would be a tight fit.

Iris wandered into one of the rear bedrooms that would become the new kitchen and looked out a window to a back yard of packed dirt. She saw a black Dodge Ram, a Harley Davidson, and Milo's BMW motorcycle parked there next to a large green dumpster. Would she ever be able to love this yard the way she loved her garden on Washington Avenue that she'd planted by hand over many years?

CHAPTER 35

The last two weeks had been the best in Rosica's life. She felt completely free and saw an exciting life ahead of her. She'd moved out of Mama's house into a sweet summer sublet on Howard Street in Cambridgeport within walking distance of Harvard Square. Rosica had used the money from Reid's savings account to pay for the apartment's upfront expenses and had given Mama her word that she'd return every day to care for the invalid before Drago got home.

Rosica viewed her trips back to East Cambridge like a part-time job, slotted between her mornings pumping iron at the gym and her late afternoons tracking Milo Miller.

Everything was ready. Her bed was neatly made with clean sheets. There were condoms in the drawer of the bedside table. She had even bought fresh daisies at the grocery store to set on top of the bureau. She changed from her jeans into the long flowered dress she'd bought on line and swirled around in front of the full-length mirror. She'd wear the dress with motorcycle boots and her black leather jacket instead of the tight-ass suede boots and cardigan that Iris Reid had worn. Rosica was the kind of woman

Milo would go for.

In the bathroom, she lined her large, green eyes with dark liner and worked some product into her strawberry blond bob to make it stand out in spikes. Then she stuffed her wallet and keys into her jacket pocket before heading out to her motorcycle.

Milo's band, Ritual Magic, was playing at a Cambridge bar at ten that evening. Through a ground-floor window of his house, Rosica had watched the band rehearse with Milo playing lead guitar and singing most of the vocals. Their music was a kind of soulful rock.

*   *   *

That morning, Rosica had scoped out the tiny bar, *Plough and Stars*, in order to plan her moves.

It was nine forty-five when she squeezed her BMW bike into half a space on Mass Ave, a block from her destination. She unhooked her helmet, respiked her hair with her fingers, and unfurled the section of her dress she'd pinned under her thighs for the ride over. The bar looked pretty busy for a Tuesday night. Maybe Milo had a following. Maybe he had groupies. The walls were tomato red and big stars dangled from the ceiling. A plough hung above the bar which ran along the whole left side of the room. Rosica could see a tiny stage at the far end of the long, narrow space. The tables near the stage were all taken so she looped her helmet through her arm and headed for a stool at the bar .

A hefty bartender with a full red beard approached. "You having dinner?"

Rosica put down the menu."Just a rum-and-Diet Coke. Myers if you have it."

"We don't have Diet Coke. You want regular?"

"Fine." She'd work off those calories later tonight.

The stage was empty except for an elaborate double keyboard, a drum kit, and several large amplifiers.

A guy in a plaid shirt on the next bar stool leaned over close enough for her to smell his yeasty beer breath. He pointed at her helmet with his chin. "You ride some kind of scooter?"

"Not exactly." She gave him a discouraging look. "Do you mind if we change places? I'm here to see the band."

He shrugged and gave her his stool. She turned away from him to face the stage.

Milo and three other musicians appeared through a back door. Milo's cool gray eyes swept the crowd and Rosica imagined that they lingered for an extra second on her. He had a bright blue electric guitar slung over one shoulder and he wore the same tight leather pants she'd seen him in at the building site, his black hair loose down his back. The drummer, keyboard player, and bass guitarist ambled to their places to adjust mics and equipment. Milo tuned his guitar.

With three sets of eyes turned to Milo for a head nod, they launched into their first song. Rosica could feel the rhythm of the music pulsing through her. The whole room came alive as people swayed and tapped to the beat. Milo's soft, melodious voice sang of frustration and loss. The bass player, a tiny hat pulled low over his glasses, harmonized with him in the chorus.

Rosica tried to catch Milo's eye, but his attention was on staying in synch with his bandmates. A sheen of sweat formed on his skin. He drank from a water bottle between songs and wiped his brow on a scarf tied around his wrist. After an hour, Milo announced their last song, something he had written for *a woman he had once loved.*

Rosica found the song painfully sad. He sang of a lover who'd had a tough life and couldn't open up to him. Milo clearly had a sensitive soul. She'd show him that a tough life hadn't hardened *her* heart. She would treat him gently. Unless, of course, he was one of the ones who relished the angst of being treated badly— who begged a woman to walk over him in stilettos. She could roll that way too.

The band set their equipment on stands and came to the bar to talk with the bartender who had four shots of clear liquid waiting for them. Rosica got up and walked closer to the inner circle. Several people, male and female, were crowded around the band members making small talk and congratulating them. She wiggled her way up next to Milo and "accidentally" bumped him with her helmet. When he turned, glanced at the helmet and then into her wide green eyes, she could tell he was interested. He flashed her a shy smile.

"That was a great set. Do you write all of your songs?"

"Most of them." His eyes crinkled as he leaned back against the bar. "I'm Milo. What's your name?"

"Rose." For the first time in her life she tried to look demure.

After a few seconds with them smiling awkwardly at each other, the bartender tapped Milo on the shoulder and handed him a thick envelope. "We've had a band cancel for Memorial Day weekend. You guys interested in the spot?"

Milo spun toward him. "Hell, yeah. Which night?"

"May twenty-seventh. Saturday, I think. Call me and we can work out the terms."

"Definitely." Milo turned back to Rose. "Sorry about the interruption. Can I buy you a drink?"

From the stage, the drummer called out."Yo, Milo. We're gonna break down the set and start loading the truck."

Milo smiled an apology. "Damn. I'd better go help them. Maybe we can get together to talk some other time?"

Rosica grabbed a napkin off the counter and, with a pen from her jacket, scribbled her name and some numbers. "This is my cell."

She folded the napkin and slid it into the front pocket of his tight leather pants, holding his eyes.

She could sense those eyes following her as she sashayed down the aisle to the front door.

CHAPTER 36

Iris answered the doorbell at her Washington Avenue house and stepped aside to let her brother enter. Sterling had his hands raised in a defensive gesture.

"Greg is still trying to track down the motorcycle. Do you have any idea how many silver Honda motorcycles there are in New England? He did discover that the tattoo on the woman you thought was following you appears to be a golden lion set against a red shield from the Bulgarian flag. That's not good news, by the way, since there are some tough Bulgarian gangs in Roxbury. Let's hope she doesn't belong to one. Also, we're negotiating with the bank's lawyers to get them to cover the money taken from your savings account, so we *are* making progress." Sterling looked from the entryway into the adjacent rooms. "You've really changed this place."

Sheba sniffed at his shiny wingtips and circled back to the kitchen.

"Actually, I didn't ask you over to discuss my case. Come in and have a seat." Iris gestured toward the living room. "Can I get you something to drink?"

Sterling froze and shot her a narrow-eyed look. "I'll bite. What's going on? Is Luc finally making you an honest woman? Hey, that might help in your defense—being settled down."

Iris sank into one of the Le Corbusier chairs. "Not exactly. Luc and I are moving in together. We'll live upstairs over his new restaurant. I was wondering if you wanted to buy this house back. Wouldn't you and Leesa love to live in the city again, closer to work?"

Sterling stared at her, then held up a righteous forefinger, stabbing the air. "Let me get this straight. When you moved back here from New York, you just *had* to have this house. You pleaded with me to sell you my share, saying the house meant so much to you. Against my better judgment, I gave in. And now you want to dump it to shack up with your boyfriend?"

"I don't want to get rid of it. I want to keep it in the family."

"Leesa and I don't want to uproot our lives. We have a perfectly nice life out in Wellesley. Why would we want to move back to Cambridge? And, no offense, but what do you think will happen if you and Luc call it quits?"

"Give me some credit, Sterling. Luc and I love each other and we're trying to move forward. Why can't you just be supportive for a change?"

"I'm trying to keep your derriere out of jail! You don't call that supportive?"

They locked eyes.

Iris blinked first. "You know what this house symbolized for me when our parents died."

"Don't give me that baloney sausage about what negligent parents we had and how the house made up for it. The statute of limitations is up. You're a middle-aged woman. Time to grow up."

Sterling stormed out, slamming the door behind him.

Iris, clasped her hands around the back of her neck and prayed that her sanctimonious brother had gotten his car towed, or at least ticketed.

CHAPTER 37

Rosica waited for Milo in a booth at the Temple Bar on Mass Ave. The Maitre d' hadn't wanted to seat her until her "whole party" was there, but Rosica had said that her 'boyfriend' was parking. Milo had suggested this bistro, saying it was close to where he was working, unaware that Rosica knew exactly where *that* was.

She glanced at the time on her phone, hoping he wouldn't be much longer. The Wednesday after-work herd was pouring in so the noise level was rising.

When Milo headed toward her table a few minutes later, Rosica watched a number of eyes, male and female, tracking him. As he approached, he slid the rubber band off his pony-tail, and shook out his long black hair. Rosica felt her pulse quickening.

He smiled and slipped into the booth. "Sorry I'm late. Things are crazy at the construction site. How're you?"

"I'm good. I just got here myself. You work in construction? The band isn't full-time?"

"I wish." Milo easily caught the waitress' eye and they ordered a Dogfish Head IPA for him and a rum-and-Diet-Coke for her.

"I'm a general contractor, renovating a house into a fancy restaurant."

"Wow, that sounds like a high-pressure job. Do you like the people you work with?"

"My crew's OK and the project's pretty cool. The architect's a little picky."

"An architect? He's the one who does the drawings—right?"

"More than that. In this case, the architect's a 'she'."

"That's unusual, isn't it?" *They were already talking about Iris Reid.*

Milo cocked his head. "I don't think I've ever worked with a female architect before."

"You said she's picky?"

"She and the owner are a couple, so she's got a personal interest. She's at the site every day."

Rosica made a pained expression. "That could be annoying."

"She's OK. They're gonna live above the restaurant, and she wants to make sure all the details are right. I like that she cares so much." Milo rested his arm over the back of the booth, revealing a snake tattoo encircling a chiseled bicep below his t-shirt sleeve. "I'm that way too. How 'bout you? Tell me about yourself."

Rosica ran a hand through her short blond hair. "I'm a kindergarten teacher in Charlestown. It's fun to work with kids that age, while they're still open and innocent, but it's exhausting, too. I'm not planning on teaching forever, so I need to figure out what I want to do next." The schoolteacher cover would provide an excuse for why she wasn't working all summer. The teachers' blogs had given her lots of background stories to throw into their conversations.

They went through several rounds of drinks, then shared a white clam pizza with a side order of calamari while discussing music, motorcycles, and where they'd grown up. After Googling Milo to confirm that he had grown up many towns away on the South Shore, Rosica had decided that she would be from Malden.

As they finished their meal, Rosica traced Milo's snake tattoo with her finger and raised an eyebrow provocatively. Milo called for the check.

Outside on the sidewalk, they both felt a little tipsy. Milo got out his phone. "I think I'll leave my bike at the job-site and call an Uber. Did you take the T to get here?"

Rosica nodded her head lazily. "Why don't we take an Uber back to my place for a night cap?"

It took mere seconds for Milo to punch the Cambridgeport address into his Uber app.

CHAPTER 38

"What do you *mean* you have to set up an investigation into these charges? I never even *applied* for this card. I only learned about it by checking my credit reports today," Iris shouted into the phone. "I filed a police report two months ago and put a freeze on my credit so this couldn't happen."

The Capital One representative with a strong Indian accent sounded like it was *his* patience that was being tried. "Please don't raise your voice, Madam. I'm trying to help you. You say that you filed a police report and credit freeze on March eighteenth but this card was approved on March seventh. The Apple computer, the Forever 21 clothes, and the Newbury Street Spa charges were put on the card on March eighth and ninth. We sent your bill in early April to the Somerville, Massachusetts address you gave us. It's now mid-May and the bill is overdue. We will, of course, put the balance of three thousand nine hundred and eighty-nine dollars and twenty two cents on hold during the duration of the investigation."

When was this Kafkaesque nightmare going to end? Iris crushed the empty water bottle on her desk with a tight fist. "I didn't buy a new computer, get my hair colored and body massaged at a spa, or buy over two thousand dollars worth of clothes at Forever 21. I've never even heard of that store and I don't live at that Somerville address. You can tell those investigators that I'm not going to pay for things that I didn't buy."

"Of course not, Madam. I'm sure they will get to the bottom of this at their earliest convenience. Do not get yourself overly heated."

The tightness in her chest made her worry she might be having a heart attack. Deep breaths. *This would be fixed. The investigators would sort out these charges.*

"OK, OK, the fraud department can straighten out the credit issues, but I want to make sure that this card is de-activated immediately."

"Yes, Madam, I can do that. But you should know that we were given all the correct information when the card was approved—social security number, mother's maiden name, etcetera. But since we have no way of knowing if the person who applied for the card is the real Iris Reid or if you are, we would prefer to close down this card just to be safe."

"*I'm* the real Iris Reid! Why would I be trying to shut down someone else's account? What possible good would that do me?"

"Maybe a personal grudge? I do not know. Nevertheless, we will shut down this card immediately, Madam. You can be sure of that."

Deep breaths. "Thank you," she said through gritted teeth as she tried to put the phone down gently. She looked down at Sheba, who eyed her warily.

"And don't call me Madam!" she shouted back to the guiltless phone.

CHAPTER 39

Within a month, Rosica and Milo were spending most of their evenings together, except for band rehearsal nights. They cooked for each other (Milo's specialty was Italian), saw movies (they both liked action flicks and she pretended to enjoy the broody art films he enjoyed), and rode their motorcycles together on weekends on Route 2 all the way out to the western part of the state.

When *Ritual Magic* had a gig, Rosica went along and sat in the audience, marveling at her luck in catching this sexy prize of a man. She could tell that most of the women in the audience wanted him too.

They stayed mainly at her apartment, which she had come to think of as "the love nest." She felt so comfortable with Milo that she sometimes had to remind herself not to let down her guard and show him who she really was. He might have wondered how this kindergarten teacher had learned to be such a tigress in bed but, who knew, maybe kindergarten teachers were all like this in the U.S.

There was no way she would ever introduce him to her family. She'd claimed she was an orphan, an only child. Milo had parents in a town called Kingston, south of Boston, but he hadn't yet brought her down to meet them.

The only place that seemed off-limits to Rosica was the construction site. Milo said it would be unprofessional for him to mix his private life with his work life. After four weeks of dating, it was starting to bother her. Apparently Iris Reid was still showing up at the site every day.

"Iris had a great idea about how to color the plaster. The additive she came up with produces a rich glow," Milo would say during dinner. Or "Iris wants us to sand and wax the floors instead of using polyurethane. It's going to give the space a roughness that will play off against the vertical onyx panels we're installing on the wall behind the bar."

Rosica couldn't picture what he was describing. She just knew that she was fed up with Milo's enthusiasm for Iris Reid's brilliance. Something had to be done to knock this bitch down a peg or two.

While she was emptying Mama's bedpan into the olive-colored toilet, an idea came to her. As soon as she got back to her apartment, she opened her laptop and typed in "examples of bad interior design." She scrolled through pictures of garden gnomes, statues of black men dressed up like jockeys, mirrored ceilings in bedrooms (*why was that considered bad taste?*), and astroturf carpets. She finally came to a chandelier that even her unschooled eyes could tell was hideous. It looked like a porcupine with purple quills dipped in glittery pink at the ends. There was a helpful link to a website where it could be purchased.

Rosica went to her bedroom and pulled down a gym bag from an upper shelf in her closet. Out of a zippered compartment she extracted one of the Iris Reid credit cards that she hadn't used yet. She hummed to herself as she made her way back to the laptop to order one of these monstrosities in Iris' name. In the space for the shipping information, she typed in the address of Milo's construction site.

CHAPTER 40

Iris stood huddled in a corner of the new restaurant's ladies room experimenting with paint colors. She was trying to capture the pale-yellow-with-a-hint-of-pink color of champagne. She would let a first layer of paint dry in one section while using a rag to create a thin, second over-wash in another section. She would build up multiple layers then wait for it to dry to see if the effect was right.

Out of the corner of her eye, she noticed Milo in the doorway.

"Come check out the Molteni range they just delivered. I've never seen anything like it."

"You mean the budget-buster? It'd better be made of solid gold." Iris straightened and stretched her back, then followed Milo down the hall.

Two of his carpenters were unpacking the range to inspect it.

"Yeah, but look at that beast," Milo said. "This is a fetishist stove."

Iris let out a whistle. The range was glossy black with brass edging and knobs. It would form the centerpiece of the kitchen and would be the oven and cooktop that Luc himself used when he was working. Ever since he'd had a Molteni range in his restaurant in Rome, he'd dreamt of having one to cook on again.

"Now I get why Luc had to have this." Iris opened the oven door to see the high-gloss red interior. "I don't even care how it cooks. We may need another one in our living room upstairs for decoration."

Milo cracked a half smile.

It was mid June and the kitchen door was propped open to let in a breeze. Iris noticed Milo's motorcycle out in the parking lot. "I've been meaning to ask you, where do you have your motorcycle serviced? Is there a garage that specializes in them?"

"I've always taken my bike to Big Bertha's in Watertown. There's nothing that woman doesn't know about motorcycles. Everyone around here goes there. Why, are you thinking of getting one?"

"I *am* looking for one. So Bertha's a real person?"

"Oh, yeah. Very real."

*　　*　　*

Later that afternoon, when Iris pulled her Jeep up to a bay at Big Bertha's and peeked in, she could tell what Milo meant. A female, plus-size version of Rod Stewart was working on a huge Harley. She had Rod's frosted shag haircut and a fake tan. Iris bet that the mole on her upper lip was self-applied. She wore blue overalls and was using a wrench to tighten something on the motorcycle which was up on a lift.

"Excuse me, hello? Are you Bertha?"

The woman pointed to the name *Bertha* in script across her ample chest and said, "You mind pulling your cage over to a space on the side?"

Iris guessed she was being asked to move the Jeep, did so, and returned to find Bertha removing the motorcycle's back wheel.

"Sorry to bother you," Iris tried again. "I'm trying to track down an old Silver Honda motorcycle driven by a young woman in her twenties. Does she service her motorcycle here?"

Bertha stared her up and down. "You a bro?"

Iris had no idea what this meant in biker context so she said, "That's right."

"This rider a patch holder or a lone wolf?"

"I'm not sure." *Damn, why didn't she bring her biker decoder ring?*

"Sorry, can't help you. Don't know that ride."

Iris had the distinct feeling that Bertha was lying.

CHAPTER 41

From her perch on a bench outside Simon's coffee shop, Rosica would be able to see when the FedEx truck arrived. She was tracking it on her laptop and the website showed it as "out for delivery," but who knew how long that could take. She was a little nervous that Milo might take a break and come over to the coffee shop, but she had noted, when she went in for her black coffee, that they didn't serve the blend of pure green Yogi decaf tea that he drank exclusively. He never drank caffeine or hard liquor. He probably considered his body a temple, and she couldn't disagree.

Rosica's cell phone rang and she looked at the Caller ID curiously.

"Bertha here, doll," said the caller unnecessarily. No one else had Bertha's gravelly, smoker's voice. "FYI, some poseur was sniffing around my place yesterday asking if I knew of a broad riding an old Silver Honda. Said she was a bro, but my mama didn't raise no fool."

"What'd she look like?"

"Tight-assed bitch, fortyish, drives a Jeep. Definitely not a bro."

"Shit. How did she find out about my ride? Did you say anything about me?"

"Whadda you think, girlfriend?"

"Thanks, Bertha. I owe you."

How had Reid learned about her ride? She'd only ridden it around the woman at the antiques warehouse, and she was sure that Reid hadn't seen her exit from that disaster. She'd have to decide how to counter this latest threat, but first, she intended to enjoy her morning's entertainment.

Rosica returned to the Bulgarian news site she'd been reading, when she spotted a delivery truck slowing to pull into the driveway. She peeked around the coffee shop's storefront as the FedEx guy dropped a huge box on the porch, rang the front doorbell, and jumped back into his front seat to race off to his next delivery.

Milo answered the door wearing a tool belt over his leather pants. *Was he going to wear those pants all summer?* He lifted the box and disappeared back inside.

Rosica sauntered casually up the driveway, past the porch, then scurried into the cover of some big bushes along the far side of the house. She peeked through a tall window into the front room, her eyes just above the floor level.

She could see the box sitting unopened, with no Milo in sight. Looks like she'd have to wait for the architect to arrive to open it.

She only hoped that Milo would be present to witness Reid lose her crown as the Queen of "brilliant" taste.

She made herself comfortable in the soft blanket of mulch and peered into the house. The building looked pretty impressive, with it's high ceilings and fancy fireplace. It was a good project for Milo. But it was time for him to stop believing that Iris Reid walked on water.

Speaking of the devil, the front door creaked open and Reid herself appeared in the entrance to the room. She walked over and examined the box, then disappeared. In a minute, she returned with Milo, who handed her a utility knife. He watched as she sliced open the box and removed a top layer of bubble wrap. Milo lifted out a huge roundish object so Reid could unwind the surrounding wrappings. He rested it down again on top of the box and backed up. They both wore horrified expressions. Reid took out the paperwork and studied it, shaking her head. She sunk down to the floor. Milo sat down next to her and said something Rosica couldn't make out. Reid started talking, gesturing with her hands, looking emotional. Milo's eyes got wider and wider. Finally, tears fell from Reid's eyes and Milo put his arm around her.

Rosica almost jumped in through the window. How had her perfect scheme backfired?

CHAPTER 42

"I can't believe I lost it in front of a contractor." Iris sat cross-legged in Ellie's front garden, letting dirt run through her fingers, sunglasses over her red-rimmed eyes.

Ellie lay down her trowel. "How did Milo react?"

"He was actually very sweet. He listened to my story about the identity theft, then put his arm around me—in a comforting way, not weird." Iris threw up her hands. "But I can't behave like that at a job site. Dammit—I've just confirmed every prejudice male contractors have about working with female architects."

"Forget that for a minute. I want to understand why you were so freaked out by getting this hideous light fixture. So, the company mixed up your order. What's the big deal?"

"I never ordered anything from this company. And it was charged to a credit card in my name that I've never seen before."

Ellie sat back on her feet. "Shit. She's still at it."

"Exactly. *She* sent the damn light. *She* knows where I work and what I do. It was one thing when she used my identity to disguise herself during the bank robbery. It was another to steal money from my savings account. Those moves at least benefitted her, but this one doesn't. Now she's made it personal."

"But why? If she were smart, she'd disappear with her ill-gotten gains. By going after you personally, she opens herself up to getting caught."

"*Why* is the question. Why does she want to jerk me around, and why would she think that sending an ugly light fixture would be the way to do that?"

Ellie rubbed her nose, smearing dirt across the bridge. "How did she even find out where you're working?"

"She must be stalking me again. I thought she'd given up after the antiques warehouse incident." Iris glanced up and down the street but saw only parked cars lining one side—no pedestrians. "Remember how I told you I sensed someone watching me while I was walking Sheba a month ago?"

"You've got to go to the police about this."

"There's nothing the police can do. They couldn't even do anything when she pushed the breakfront over and almost killed me. She's a ghost. They won't be able to find her."

"What's this woman's end game? Sending you a light fixture that you can just return is a time-consuming nuisance, but nothing more."

"Maybe she's putting me on notice that she knows everything about my life, what I do, where I work. She's harmed me in concrete ways and now she's messing with my head."

"What a friggin' psycho."

CHAPTER 43

Cradling a bag of groceries, Iris let herself and her dog into Luc's condo at lunchtime to find him on his stomach on the living room carpet in his boxer-briefs, his hands gripping his ankles.

Sheba trotted over to lick his face.

Luc gave the dog a kiss and scrambled up. "Plough pose. Great for my back." He shrugged his shoulders up and down. "I wish I'd discovered yoga earlier. You should come to these classes. Hannah is amazing."

"Maybe I will someday. That means never."

Luc slipped on a t-shirt. "Don't dis it 'til you try it. None of us are getting any younger."

Iris shot out a roundhouse kick, tapping him on the solar plexus. "Speak for yourself."

He grabbed the bag from her as they headed toward the kitchen, then started unpacking it on the island, eyeing the contents. He held up a pineapple and sniffed its bottom. "Mmmm...ripe."

Iris put a bottle of Cava in the freezer. "I'm making Pad Krapow Moo Saap."

"I don't have a wok."

"I can improvise." She lined up the waxed paper packages of minced pork, oyster sauce, and red chilis on the counter, then located the remaining ingredients in the fridge.

"How's my new restaurant coming along?" Luc asked.

Iris gave him a progress report as she chopped and assembled garlic and chilies, tossing them into a bowl. Then she told him about the light fixture incident.

Luc retrieved the Cava from the freezer, gently eased out the cork, and poured some into glasses. He handed Iris a flute and sat on a stool at the island, watching her lift a cast iron pan onto a burner and heat up some peanut oil. "You think the bank robber ordered it? That's bizarre. How did she know where to send it?"

Iris tossed the pork into the pan and stirred it as it sizzled in the hot oil. "I think she followed me. I told Lieutenant Choi about it, and Greg Perrelli. They were both encouraged by the fact that the woman is still hanging around, playing mind games with me. They said this will give them more of a chance to catch her."

"Swell—they're not the one being stalked. Why is she still messing with you?"

"Everything was quiet for weeks. I keep wondering whether I did something to escalate things in her sick little mind."

Luc fingered the stem of his Cava glass. "Can you think of anything that might have set off her alarms?"

"I did go to a place in Watertown that Milo told me services motorcycles and asked the owner if she knew a young woman who rides an old silver Honda. She said no, but I had a feeling she was lying."

"It's dangerous for you to try to catch this woman yourself. If Ms. Honda was a long-time customer, the owner could have warned her that you were looking for her and knew about her bike. That would have freaked her out big time. You need to let Choi or Perrelli confront her."

"Choi said she'd interview Bertha, the garage owner, but that they couldn't stake out the place 24/7 waiting for Ms. Honda to turn up. They've already been looking for the motorcycle for several months."

"Maybe we need to exert a little pressure on Bertha ourselves. Make it worth her while to help us find the bike's owner. I know that Sterling says he feels confident about the case, but this is the closest we've come to actually catching this psycho. We need to trap her."

"What'd you have in mind, tough guy? Gonna rough up big Bertha?"

Luc grinned. "You think I can't take her on? Exactly how big is Bertha?"

"Much as I'd love to watch that scene, I think I've got a better idea."

* * *

After lunch, Iris made a phone call. As soon as she heard Budge Buchanan's whiny voice she wondered what she'd been thinking, intentionally getting him involved.

"What a delightful surprise, Reid. What's on your mind?"

"As I'm sure you remember, my case is coming up next month. Given all the front-page ink you've devoted to the story, I was wondering if you'd be interested in an exclusive interview with me."

"A confession?"

"Don't get your hopes up."

"When and where? But not one of those impossible-to-park-at places that you favor in Harvard Square."

"I walk or take the T like a responsible urbanite. You're not out in the sticks of New Hampshire anymore, Buchanan."

Budge and Iris had been classmates at Dartmouth many years before and their interactions in the Boston area hadn't made Iris any fonder of him than she'd been back then. But sometimes he was useful.

"Meet me at Bagelsaurus on Mass Ave near Porter Square at ten tomorrow morning. Just you. No recordings, no cameras."

CHAPTER 44

"Of course you trust Luc," Ellie said as she threw a pair of gym shorts and a sleeveless T-shirt into her gym bag while Iris watched idly from the edge of Ellie's bed. "Now where did I leave my yoga mat?"

"I'm not going to be *that* woman, the insecure one who's always checking up on her man." Iris gulped from her water bottle and wiped her mouth on her sleeve. "We're supposed to hydrate before class."

"Think of this as trying out a new hobby that you might want to share with Luc. He's been raving about how good these classes make him feel, right? So, you're giving it a try, being supportive." Ellie slung the bag's strap over a shoulder. "Did you tell him we're coming?"

Iris grabbed her own yoga bag. "No, I just cleared it with Hannah. She said to get there by five-thirty to fill out forms."

* * *

Ten minutes later, they sat on beanbag chairs in the yoga

studio's anteroom initialing endless releases on a pair of clipboards..."not liable"... "no heart problems"... "if you pass out".

Hannah, half-naked in her sports bra and tiny lycra shorts, was running through the etiquette and expectations for their first Bikram class. "It's important to stay in the room for the entire ninety minutes. It's OK if you need to rest, but follow along when you can. Don't drink until I tell you it's OK. After that you may take sips during the intervals between asanas. There's no talking during the class but you can ask me questions afterward."

Iris pulled her hair back into an elastic, "Ellie and I do yoga all the time. I'm sure we'll be fine. How hot did you say the room is?"

"105 degrees of wet heat. Did you bring towels?"

Iris and Ellie exchanged panicked looks.

"No worries." Hannah passed them two towels from a shelf behind her desk. "The locker room is through that door. Class starts in ten minutes."

Entering the studio felt like walking into a blast furnace. Iris spotted Luc, stretching out his quads on a mat in the front row closest to the mirrors. His eyes widened when he noticed her setting up her mat next to Ellie's in the back row. She gave him a little wave.

The small room was packed—twelve people in three rows—only one guy other than Luc, a tall redhead with a man bun. In the suffocating heat, Iris felt overdressed in her long Yoga pants and baggy cotton T-shirt. Most of the fit-looking women were dressed like Hannah; the two men were shirtless and wearing gym shorts. The room smelled like overcooked, stale sweat. *Was someone going to check on the heat? This temperature couldn't be right, could it? When did I last shave my legs? Just stretch like everyone else. Act yoga-ish.*

Iris smiled at the middle-aged woman in a shiny pink shortie suit whose mat was wedged in next to hers. "Namaste," Iris whispered, bowing her head slightly.

The woman shushed her and glared.

Hannah floated to the front of the class wearing an irritatingly tranquil expression. She instructed them to do something called Pranayama breathing, which Iris figured must mean Praying Mantis breathing since the noise sounded like angry bugs. After ten minutes, sweat was dripping into Iris' eyes and rolling down her back and between her breasts. And they'd barely begun moving.

There were two small windows high up on the side wall next to Ellie, closed tight. Was it any cooler over there? How soon until the designated water break? Did she really need to pee or was she just imagining it?

Hannah led them in a set of standing asanas, starting with Eagle pose. Iris contorted her limbs while trying to perform the one-legged squat without falling over. The now-sodden towel on her mat was slippery. Hannah was pulling off the graceful bird-of-prey look while Iris resembled a quivering snake. Hannah's skin merely glistened while Iris' sweat had drenched her T-shirt and long pants. Her hair was plastered inelegantly to her head. She felt like she was moving through molasses.

As the class moved together into a wide leg forward bend, Iris' face was inches from the intimidating rear end directly in front of her. Several moves later, they relaxed into a much-needed Shavasana, or corpse pose, after which Hannah finally allowed them to take a water break. Ellie gave Iris a *what-were-we-thinking* look while they drank. Iris rationed her water consumption, recognizing that, yes indeed, she definitely had to pee. She consulted her very slow-running watch, then caught Luc's eyes in the mirror. He winked at her, looking amused.

Iris tried to distract herself from her protesting bladder by counting the number of animal or insect poses in Yoga. She moved through the Cobra and Locust with her muscles shaking and her arms tingling with pins and needles. As if it were possible, the room seemed to have gotten hotter. By the time the class proceeded into Ustrasana, a back bend, she felt almost delirious.

Hannah padded over to Luc and rested her palm under his back, lifting him gently for more of a stretch. Their ponytails were the same shade of blond. Hannah had a look of enlightened bliss on her face.

Iris' hands skidded on the wet towel and she landed head-first on the floor. All eyes turned to stare as she collected her towel and mat and left the room with as much dignity as she could muster.

ROSICA

CHAPTER 45

Rosica bustled around the love nest, setting the table and repeatedly checking on the chicken in the oven. It was an especially hot June evening and the apartment was sweltering. It had been foolish to cook indoors on an evening like this, but she was determined to produce a home-cooked dinner. Hadn't Milo called her his "domestic goddess" just the week before? She dialed the window air conditioner in the bedroom up to its highest setting and left the door open.

Rosica had taken the T from Cambridgeport to her vigil at Milo's construction site that morning. She was glad she hadn't ridden her motorcycle anywhere near Iris Reid's turf after Bertha's warning. For that matter, now even the Cambridge police might be looking for it. She had it under a tarp in the back yard, but Milo would wonder why she wasn't using it. Maybe she could replace it with something newer and tell him she wanted a better ride. But she loved her old Honda. She'd gotten it when she'd first arrived in Cambridge and it had been her way to escape from life with her crazy, infuriating family. Having to ditch her ride was just one more way that Iris Reid was screwing up her life.

Would Milo tell her about the delivery of the ugly light? Would he confide in Rosica or be protective of Reid? Milo was not an open kind of guy in general, and lately, she had sensed him pulling away. Or was that her imagination?

She checked the time. Milo would show up any minute now. She ran into the bedroom to change into a tight T-shirt and jeans shorts. She gelled her blond hair up into spikes and added heavy eyeliner. Milo liked her rocker chick look.

Her curiosity would be hard to keep in check while she waited for him to bring up the subject of the morning's episode with Reid, but she needed to play it cool. Still, she was dying to know if he'd lost respect for Reid when she'd started to cry. That was weak. Rosica couldn't believe that a woman like her would cry at work. But maybe she did it on purpose to get him on her side. She probably told him about this mean bitch doing things to her, then cried to get his sympathy. Reid was so manipulative.

Her phone buzzed. It was Milo. "Hey, babe," Rosica cooed. "You on your way?"

There was a pause. "I think I'll just head home tonight. It's been an intense day. You don't mind, do you?"

"Sure you don't want to come talk about it? I know some ways to relieve your tension."

"Maybe tomorrow. I'm beat."

"OK, that's cool." As Rosica lay down the phone she smelled something starting to burn.

CHAPTER 46

Iris was seated at a small table off to the side of the tiny Bagelsaurus shop by the time Budge, having taken his sweet time, strolled in. A cup of room-temperature coffee and a green bagel sat at his place. He gave her an unconvincing smile.

Iris motioned toward the seat and folded her hands in front of her. "I'd like to give you a chance to make it up to me for that photo you ran in March."

"You want me to take another photo? You said no cameras." He lifted the bagel to sniff it. "What flavor is this?"

"Vegetable."

He dropped it and moved the plate away.

Pushing aside the image of Budge as the unpleasant toad he so resembled, Iris got down to business. "You know that one of the bank robbers bears a striking resemblance to me and set me up to get arrested for her crime."

Budge examined his fingernails. "So your attorney says."

"I was able to track down the type of motorcycle my impersonator rides and where she gets it serviced. The police can't watch the place 24/7, but if you had someone who could keep an eye on the place, you might be able to break open this story about identity theft, robbery, and murder."

"What am I, the *Globe Spotlight* team? I don't have the resources for full-time surveillance. And why should I believe that this "young woman" you've dug up had anything to do with the robbery?"

Iris walked him through the story, from the Somerville neighbor, to the church in Arlington which collects donated computers, to Big Bertha's garage in Watertown. "Imagine this— another William Buchanan front page story with the twist that you, the ace reporter, are the one who actually locates the beautiful getaway driver in the infamous bank robbery where a guard got killed and the robbers vanished into thin air, followed by an exclusive interview with the femme fatale motorcycle rider that reveals what makes her tick."

"How do you know Biker Girl's a looker?"

"Pat attention! She's been described as looking like a *slightly* younger version of me."

Budge arched an eyebrow and leaned back in his plastic chair, its hind legs flexing in a worrisome way. "Hmmm, I like the plot...could be Pulitzer material."

He brought the seat upright with a wobbly thud. "But I prefer an exclusive about getaway girl's *victim* who cleverly pieces together the clues that the cops have missed and then tracks B.G. down herself. Call me when you spot her at the garage. And Iris..."

"What?

"Be careful. Biker Girl could be dangerous." Budge slid an arm back into the sleeve of his coat. "And for the record, I'm a cinnamon-raisin-bagel guy."

CHAPTER 47

Rosica tapped her fingers on the kitchen table and stared down through the window at the lumpy shape of her covered motorcycle. The previous evening, when Milo had finally come over after work, he'd asked why her bike wasn't in the driveway. She'd made up an excuse, saying that it needed new mufflers. She'd explained that Bertha hadn't been able to give her a new inspection sticker and that she was waiting for the parts to come in. Now, she needed to think of some way to get it off the road for good as soon as possible.

Milo had mentioned nothing about Reid's breakdown over the light fixture no matter how many openings Rosica had given him, asking about the "intense day" that had kept him away. That was a bad sign. Reid was starting to come between them.

Rosica scrolled through her cell contacts and tapped on Bertha's contact number.

"That you, Rosica?"

"Yup. I've got to do something about that bitch trying to track me down through my bike."

"You want me to recommend some muscle?"

"No, not for now anyway, thanks. I think I need to get rid of my old Honda. Buy something new. Do you know of any chop shops that could use a donor? And have you heard of any good bikes for sale? Something German or Japanese. No hogs."

"To each his own. I've got a Bark-o-lounger, a Honda Gold Wing, the owner wants to sell. It's a real cherry if you like that kind of thing. But I thought you loved that old piece of crap you ride. Why don't you just get it painted? If they're looking out for a silver one, paint it black. That's always a slick color.

Rosica thought about it. She closed her eyes and pictured herself riding her good old Honda, freshly-painted black. She'd get her freedom back and be invisible to the cops.

"How much?" she asked, eyes still shut.

"I could do a quick-and-dirty for a few hundred bucks." Bertha belted out a smoker's cough. "Wait, does this chick know your license plate?"

"If she did she'd have had the cops out at my mother's place by now."

"Cops. I don't want no trouble."

"No, no, she just stole something from me and I messed up her apartment a little."

"Oh, that kind of shit. "

"Still, I don't want her tracking me."

"I've got some license plates off a donor I can sell you. Bring your bike in early Thursday afternoon. I need at least a day to do a decent job."

"I owe you again, Berth."

Problem solved. Now she just needed to give Milo a credible reason for why she'd had her bike painted. *Wasn't it a woman's prerogative to want a change now and then?*

CHAPTER 48

Two mornings later, Rosica ran into Drago on the staircase at Mama's house. At ten a.m. he was lurching down, dressed only in his boxers, as she eased past him on her way up.

"Classy look, Bro. Sleeping in on a Thursday?"

"I quit that shitty job. It's time you and I got our share of the money we earned."

Rosica turned to face him. "Did Mama say she's ready to give it to us?"

"Georgi already got his share to buy that crappy farm house. Why should *we* have to keep waiting? If you and I go in there together, what can she do? She wouldn't be alive if we weren't taking care of her."

Rosica sat down on a carpeted step. "This might not be the best time. You know that broad we got the I.D. off of? She's been nosing around, starting to figure things out."

"Are you kidding? You didn't think to tell me this sooner?"

"I've got it under control. I think."

Drago sunk onto another step. "Tell me every goddamned thing."

Rosica told him about Iris' trip to the church trying to track down her old computer, as well as her visit to Big Bertha's to ask about Rosica's motorcycle. "But Helen and Bertha didn't tell her anything. Besides, I'm getting my bike painted a new color today and getting new plates with no link to me."

"How did she find out about your bike? Do the cops know about this?"

"Helen and Bertha haven't been approached by any cops so I think she's playing girl-detective on her own. She's got that court case coming up so she's got a good reason to try to find us. If the cops have bought our frame-up then they're not going to pay much attention to Reid's story about an impersonator who got away."

"I thought we were in the clear." Drago rubbed the stubble on his chin. "Now, we may have to go to ground thanks to this broad. If she's seen your bike she may have already seen your plate number. That's registered here to Mama's house, right?"

"Yeah, but if she knew that, she'd have shown up here by now."

Drago gave her a grim look. "You willing to stake all our futures on that? This bitch could be slowly working around us, tightening the noose. If the cops get ahold of this address, they can find out about all four of us."

"Then maybe it's time to move on. Get our money and split to different parts of the country. Maybe to Canada." Rosica felt a pang as she thought about leaving Milo behind.

"Oh, man, I was just starting to like it here," Drago said. "And what a hassle to move Mama. We'd have to leave this house just after we got it paid off. You've really screwed us over with your computer scams and riding around on that motorcycle, just asking to be noticed."

"Screw you. We needed to steal someone's identity to get the getaway car, or were you going to use your own credit card? If she'd seen my license plate she would have been trying to trace it instead of nosing around Bertha's asking about a chick who rode an old silver Honda bike."

"So what? We sit here like ducks, clutching our rosaries?"

Rosica bowed her head, thinking. "Let's meet here tonight, all four of us, to make a plan. You call Georgi and make sure he shows up. I'll tell Mama what's going on and that we need our shares now."

"Yeah, you get to break it to the old lady—about the danger you've put us in."

CHAPTER 49

Iris felt slightly ridiculous. She was huddled in Ellie's Volvo with a baseball cap pulled low on her forehead like a gumshoe in a Robert B. Parker novel, watching Big Bertha's garage through a pair of binoculars.

Who was she kidding? The odds that Biker Girl would bring in her motorcycle for service on this particular Thursday were slim. Iris should be experimenting with paint colors back at the restaurant, or walking Sheba, or doing anything else that might actually be productive. Then again, this might be her only shot at proving her innocence.

She turned off a tedious political discussion on NPR and yawned. The car's clock read 1:07. She'd stay here until three, if she could make it that long without a bathroom break, then maybe try again tomorrow.

Damn that Budge. *He* should be doing this. She knew he'd want the biker girl exclusive gift-wrapped for him. But, to be fair, it was *her* neck on the line.

Iris extracted a baggie from her purse, pulled it open, and bit off the corner of a tuna fish sandwich. She opened her window and fanned her hand back-and-forth. She'd have to air out the smell before she returned the car to Ellie.

Her mind wandered back to the previous day when the rental broker had brought over a couple interested in renting her house for a year, starting in September. Iris had passed them in the entry hall on her way out. Behind the eager-eyed parents trailed two bored-looking teenagers, a girl and a boy.

As Iris chewed, she remembered the look on the girl's sullen face as she'd glanced around at Iris' home. She didn't want that girl living in her home—touching her stuff, spilling nail polish in the vanity drawers, screaming down the staircase at her mother. There was no room for these strangers' inevitable domestic dramas unfolding in her house.

As she took another bite of sandwich, her gloomy thoughts were interrupted by the stuttering metallic sound of a garage door opening. She looked up. Ms. Rod Stewart, a.k.a. Big Bertha, emerged, a cigarette dangling from her mouth. Still wearing heavy gold chains over her mechanic's jumpsuit, an interesting fashion choice, Bertha dragged a large yellow sign reading "CLOSED" out to the side of her driveway. She weighted down the base of the sign with a couple of old cinderblocks, then looked up and down Arsenal Street. As Bertha trudged back to the garage, she turned and flipped the bird at the Volvo.

Swell. Busted. Bertha must have put up the "closed" sign to warn Biker Girl to stay away. But that meant she expected B.G. to be there soon. Why couldn't Bertha just call to warn her? Maybe B.G. couldn't answer her cell phone if she was already riding her motorcycle. Iris sat up taller and watched Arsenal Street through her binoculars as she finished her sandwich and worked her way through a second baggie of tart apple slices. The lights remained on inside the garage and she could make out Bertha's frosted shag moving around.

Things were getting interesting.

CHAPTER 50

Rosica had smeared mud on her license plate as a precaution but still felt exposed when she left for Bertha's that afternoon. As she rode through Harvard Square, a police car came up alongside her. They waited together at a red light, Rosica's engine grumbling at idle. The cop's eyes stared straight ahead, not at her but, after the light turned green, she veered off onto the closest side street. The pounding in her ears ebbed as she watched the cruiser disappear in her mirror.

Why was she so stupid? She'd jeopardized the whole family's safety by stalking Iris Reid, raiding her savings account, even jerking the woman around with that ugly light fixture prank. She'd made it personal—a cardinal sin in any grift. Mama had spent most of the morning saying as much, brutally lecturing Rosica from her bed. For a woman in the final stages of cancer, Mama hadn't lost her ability to intimidate.

If only she'd left Reid alone after the bank robbery, a "one and done" as they called it in the business, they wouldn't have to leave town now. She wouldn't have to leave Milo and the love nest behind. Leave the best life she'd ever had.

But maybe she was overreacting. Maybe painting her bike and changing the plates would prevent Reid from getting any closer, and Rosica could keep moving toward the future she'd allowed herself to dream about.

She waited at the light to cross Fresh Pond Parkway. She didn't see any more cops but they often lurked a half-block back on Mount Auburn Street, looking to issue their quota of tickets. She decided to hang a left and follow the Charles River instead, taking a longer route to Bertha's. The traffic was dense but that gave her cover.

At Arsenal Street she peeled off from the river and headed toward Watertown Square, passing endless car dealerships and strip malls along the way. After a mile or two, she could see the orange Big Bertha's sign up ahead on the side of a squat concrete building, but there was something yellow propped up in the driveway, a sign on a stand. As Rosica rode closer, she could read it: "CLOSED."

WTF? Bertha was expecting her. Maybe her friend had closed the shop so she could focus on the paint job. She slowed, trying to decide whether to pull into the driveway, when a sharp flash of light caught her eye. It came from a blue station wagon parked in an empty lot next to Bertha's. Rosica could see a black shadowy figure sitting in the front seat holding something reflective. *Plain-clothes detective?*

Rosica twisted the throttle wide open and made a hard turn, planting a foot briefly on the pavement. She skirted a row of cars stopped at a red light, banked a hard right onto School Street without pausing and checked her mirrors to see if the blue car was following. There it was—driving in the breakdown lane past the waiting cars and turning at the light to pursue her. She rolled on the throttle and raced ahead.

Passing the Church of the Little Lamb on her right, she considered darting into their driveway and hiding inside, but a quick check told her that the blue car was closing in too fast. Ahead, a woman was leading a little boy across the street. When Rosica slowed down to avoid hitting them, she noticed drops of rain beading on her visor. In the mirror she saw the blue car slow down briefly for the pedestrians, then race forward.

The rain was starting to come down harder. At the top of the hill, several cars were stopped at a red light at the Mount Auburn Street intersection. Rosica cranked the gas and raced past them on the right, breathing hard now, setting up for the a right-hand turn at the corner. *Too hard on her brakes. Damn!* They locked, the rear wheel skittering out wide, and she crossed up her front wheel in an attempt to recover control. She was dumping her bike—such a rookie move. Then she heard the sound of howling, sliding tires and a screaming horn.

CHAPTER 51

Iris saw Biker Girl pass a row of cars on the right and disappear into the intersection. Through the Volvo's open window, she heard the sickening crunch of metal crashing against metal.

She pulled to the side of the road and ran toward the noise. Other drivers opened their doors to see what was happening. A woman screamed. Iris ran faster.

A groan escaped her as she saw the full scope of the collision. The motorcycle was wedged under the front wheel of an SUV and Biker Girl lay on her back nearby not moving, her body caught between the tank and the handlebars. The dazed-looking man inside the SUV was pinned by his deployed air bag. Iris thought she might vomit.

Kneeling over Biker Girl, a gray-haired man with an authoritative voice said, "I'm a doctor. Can you hear me? Don't try to move. An ambulance is coming." The doctor lay his finger on her neck to feel for a pulse.

Iris barely registered that she was getting soaked. *This woman might die because she had chased her into traffic.*

She moved closer and tried to see the woman's face.

"I'm going to lift your visor now." The doctor continued. "Stay very still." He carefully unlatched and raised the face protector.

Iris gasped. She saw her own features, as if she were the one on the ground.

Rosica's panicked eyes latched onto Iris' face.

* * *

The rain had stopped by the time the EMTs arrived and extricated Rosica from the carcass of her bike. They unzipped her denim jacket, which had ridden up around her chest. There was a lot of blood on her T shirt. They worked on her for ten minutes, struggling to get an IV into her arm, then strapped her onto a stretcher, leaving her helmet in place. Iris heard one of them mutter, "Might be internal bleeding or a concussion," before they carried her to the ambulance, secured the stretcher, slammed the rear doors shut, and drove off.

The SUV driver had been taken away in another ambulance, but his injuries seemed to be mainly psychological. "She came out of nowhere. I tried to stop," he kept repeating to the Watertown police officers who'd quickly shown up after the crash.

Iris called Sterling but was told that he was in court and could not take any calls. As guilty as she felt about her role in the accident, she needed Beverley Choi at the Cambridge Police Department to know right away about this victim's connection to the bank robbery so the police could hold her and track down her accomplices. When Iris was patched through to the detective, she explained what had happened. Choi summoned her to the station to give a statement. As Iris was heading back to her car, her cell phone rang.

"I heard about a woman crashing her motorcycle in Watertown. Was it Biker Girl?" Budge's voice quavered with excitement.

"Yeah," Iris tried to keep her voice steady. "She showed up at Bertha's on the silver Honda, and was about to turn into the driveway, but she spotted me and sped off. I tailed her, she ran a red light, and got hit by an SUV."

Budge sucked in a breath. "Did you get her plate number so we can find out who she was?"

Iris exploded. "Why don't you ask if she's still alive?"

"Is she still alive?"

"Barely. And no, I haven't had the heart to try to read the license plate on the crumpled mess of her bike."

"Look, Reid, this is the woman who set you up to take the fall for a robbery and murder, then cleaned out your bank account. She didn't have to run from you or blast through a red light. You're not responsible for this." Budge paused. "Now go get me her license plate number."

Iris turned around with a sigh and headed back toward the smashed vehicles. A uniformed officer diverting traffic eyed her suspiciously. "Nothing to see here," he barked.

Iris slipped her phone into the front pocket of her shorts and meandered casually over to a spot on the sidewalk where she had a view of the back of the bike. Turning away from the cop, she whispered into the phone, "HM4417, Massachusetts plate."

"Good. Now take a photo of the crash site with your phone."

"There's a cop here guarding the area."

"Stay on the sidewalk and zoom in on the motorcycle."

Iris pinch-enlarged her screen, then pivoted around to quickly take a few shots. She jogged back to her car. When she was safely inside the Volvo, she sent the photos to Budge.

CHAPTER 52

Iris spent the rest of that afternoon at Cambridge Police headquarters. After she'd gone over her story several times, on the record, to Lieutenant Choi—how she'd tracked down the bank robber with the silver Honda motorcycle and tailed her to the Watertown crash site—Choi disappeared from the interview room for half an hour. When Choi returned, she placed a file in front of Iris on the table and said, "It was foolish of you to attempt surveillance on your own. This wasn't a job for an amateur. I could arrest you for reckless endangerment, for chasing this woman."

Iris sat up in her chair indignantly. "Would you have been willing to have your detectives watch Big Bertha's garage indefinitely? *I'm* the one being accused of this woman's crime. If I couldn't produce this imposter, you might have sent me to jail."

Choi held up both hands. "I'm not going to arrest you. Since the crash victim chose to flee before you started to pursue her, we won't be pressing charges." She slid a sheaf of papers across the table. "Please sign your statement for both the Cambridge and Watertown police departments, then you're free to leave."

As Iris went to retrieve the Volvo, hoping she'd avoided a

ticket at the expired meter, her phone pinged. A text from Budge read "Meet me in your driveway at five." That gave her just enough time to drop off Ellie's car in Cambridge.

When she rounded the corner of Arlington Street and jogged the gentle slope down Washington Avenue, she saw Budge's tiny Fiat 500 in her driveway. As she got close, Budge pushed open the passenger door and Iris wedged herself inside, twisting sideways to face him. "Did you find out who she is?"

Budge held up a finger as he took several minutes to finish texting something on his phone. After he pressed send, he sat back in his seat, looking smug. "Another Buchanan front-page story."

Iris thought she might just strangle him. "Who is she?"

"The photo you took's gonna be on the front page too. I'll make a good source of you yet."

Iris grabbed his shoulders and started to shake him.

Budge wriggled loose. "Chill." He scrolled down on his phone, then held up an official-looking photo of the woman with green eyes. "Recognize her?"

Iris looked closely. "The resemblance is really creepy. Our features are the same."

"But she's young."

Iris smacked Budge across the chest.

"OK, younger. Is that better?"

Iris handed back the phone. "Who is she?"

"The paper ran her license plate," Budge continued. "It was registered to a Rosica Bakalov. The address listed is a house in East Cambridge owned by a woman in her late 50s, name of Grozda Bakalov. Emigrated from Bulgaria four years ago with her three adult children, two sons and a daughter—your biker friend, Rosica, I guess."

Iris let out a deep breath. "That's them—the bank robbers. Thank God they're caught."

"Uh, not so fast. I got to the house while the cops were searching it. They wouldn't let me in, natch, but I could tell from the vibe that the coop had been flown."

"No! How could the family have known that the police were on to them?"

"I learned from the cop on the door that there was a police scanner in an upstairs bedroom. It looks like the mother was bedridden and spent her time watching TV and listening to the scanner. She must have heard about the accident and put the pieces together. They took off in a rush, leaving everything behind, so the police should be able to learn a lot about them. There's a BOLO out with pictures from their IDs so, hopefully, they'll be captured soon."

Iris smiled without warmth. "I'd love to have seen Lieutenant Choi's face when she learned that I really did have a doppelgänger." Iris rubbed the back of her neck. "Can you find out for me what Rosica Bakalov's condition is?"

CHAPTER 53

Georgi sat in the barely furnished living room, staring out through a dusty picture window as dusk settled in on the front yard. A lot of weeds out there. Thank God Mama had recently let him buy this old farm house in Abington, using cash and one of the fake IDs. He knocked back the last drops from the tall can of Narragansett.

Periodically, Mama's shrill voice cackled forth from the next room, now her makeshift bedroom with little more than a mattress on the floor.

"When is Drago coming back with my TV? I can't believe you idiots left my police scanner behind," Mama whined for the umpteenth time since they'd fled East Cambridge, only hours before.

"Would you rather be sitting in a jail cell now?" Georgi snapped back. Mama was not getting the picture. She was too far gone with the cancer to help them with any kind of a getaway plan. Her only daughter was in the hospital, maybe even dead. You'd think she'd be a bit concerned about that. Who'd she think was going to change her bedpans now?

His phone buzzed and he saw that it was his girlfriend, Charleen. Finally. "So, is she still alive?"

"Yeah, I told them I was her sister, like you said, but they told me she was in the ICU having emergency surgery. They wouldn't give me any more details over the phone."

Georgi stroked his bottom lip distractedly. "Babe, do you think you could go down there to Mount Auburn to talk with the docs after she's out of surgery? I'd go myself but I have to stay here with Mama."

A moment went by. "I don't know, Georgi. It's dinner time and I'm hungry. Who knows when they'll start or how long they'll be working on her."

"I'll make it worth your while, I promise. Just get yourself a couple of slices of pizza in the Square and some magazines to read, then wait until the docs can give you some news, ok? This is my sister we're talking about."

"OK, fine. But you're paying for the magazines."

He got another can of beer from the fridge, which was otherwise pretty empty. For months they'd gotten away clean from the bank robbery, and then—poof—the cops were on their tail. This fuck-up was the Reid woman's fault. She must have tracked down Rosica's bike somehow. Mama heard about the accident on the scanner. Reid must have chased Rosica into traffic and she'd gotten pasted by an SUV. The cops probably got Mama's address from the bike's license plate. Mama said Immigration records would tell the cops about the whole family, so now they had to lie low, or even split up, maybe move somewhere far away. Shit. He was just starting to get to a good place with Charleen.

Georgi felt a surge of relief when he heard Drago's truck sputtering up the dirt driveway. He tossed his empty beer cans into the kitchen trash can and headed outside.

Drago was struggling to lift an enormous cardboard box out of the truck's bed.

"Lemme help. Did you have any trouble?" Georgi asked his brother.

Drago didn't seem to hear him. He was shaking his head and muttering, "Our goddamned pictures are on TV. Our driver's license photos were plastered all over a wall of giant TVs at Best Buy. It's lucky the sales guy was dumb-as-a-stone and didn't recognize me."

CHAPTER 54

In the long hours after the accident, Rosica passed in and out of consciousness. When lucid, she could remember time slowing down as she hit the SUV, and her body flying sideways through the air until she was wedged under the car with tiny pieces of shatterproof glass floating past her face so slowly that she could see the individual blocks. Lying in the street, she felt a heavy weight weighing down on her ribcage with her legs trapped under her broken bike, but adrenaline had masked the pain. Her head inside the helmet had felt hot, and a doctor was crouched beside her, telling her to squeeze his hand. Then, she'd imagined she'd seen Iris Reid staring down at her.

Once in the operating room, Rosica was knocked out. She woke up much later in a hospital bed, her ribs feeling as if molten lead had been poured over them. She yelled, "Nurse—I need some help!"

A harried-looking nurse with weak-tea-colored skin bustled in and, before the door swung closed, Rosica noticed a uniformed cop sitting in a chair in the hallway facing her door.

"Awake, are we? How are we feeling?" the nurse asked.

"I'm in terrible pain." Rosica's voice sounded raspy to her.

The nurse consulted a clipboard hung at the base of the bed. "You had a nerve block in the E.R. But it's probably wearing off. The doctor says you can have two Percocet every four hours. I'll get them."

After Rosica had swallowed the pills and sipped some water, she asked, "What happened to me?"

The nurse checked her chart, "Your orthopedic surgeon, Doctor Kumar, took a chest x-ray and a CT scan. You fractured rib #8 and your legs have a lot of bruising. Hon, you got busted up pretty badly. Still, your lungs didn't get punctured, so that's the good news." She flipped over the sheet to read the second page. "Your right leg is heavily bruised and your torso got real scraped up—they call it road rash in these motorcycle crashes."

Rosica lifted the thin hospital sheet, raised her hospital gown, and stared at the angry red marks up and down her stomach. They itched and burned. There was a purple stripe at the site of her damaged rib. No wonder she couldn't get into a comfortable position. She dropped the sheet and focused on her torso. "Shouldn't my rib be bandaged up?"

The nurse regarded her sympathetically. "We don't do that anymore with ribs. It's more important that you're able to breath deeply. It'll take time to heal. You're lucky you didn't get a chipped elbow or broken wrist. We see that all the time with these kinds of accidents."

"Will I have any permanent damage?"

"Doctor Kumar will be stopping by in the morning and I'm sure he can answer all of your questions." With that the nurse retreated from the room.

Rosica tried to get a look at the cop as the door swung open. He stared back at her. Was he there to keep people out or to keep her in?

Either way, she was screwed. Not only was her rib messed up, but the cops must have traced her license plate by now, which would have led them to Mama's house. She was trapped and had led the cops to her family. They would all be charged for the bank robbery and would end up in jail.

She rolled to her side and cried quietly. How could Reid possibly have tracked her down?

She slipped off into a drugged sleep.

GEORGI

CHAPTER 55

At the farmhouse, Georgi knocked and then opened the door to see if Drago was in the bathroom. Empty. He rushed outside to look for the truck, the screen door banging behind him. Gone. In the kitchen he tried to phone Drago's cell, but the call went straight to voice mail.

Georgi crept into Mama's "bedroom" in the former dining room, set apart from the living room by a curtain strung across the wide opening. Images flickered across the TV screen, but the sound had been turned down low. Georgi stared at the sleeping form of his mother, curled up on the mattress on the floor. All that was left of her was a shriveled woman, prematurely older than her 59 years, spending her remaining days taunting her wretched children and complaining about the unfairness of her life.

Georgi held his breath as he slid his hand under the mattress near Mama's outstretched arm. He froze when he saw her fingers twitch, but her eyes didn't open. She let out a snort and turned onto her side, away from him. He pinched a corner of the satin pillow case filled with their money and dragged it toward him. Clutching it to his side, he tiptoed out of the room.

Georgi stacked the bills into seven $50,000 piles on the kitchen table. When he was done counting, he could see that Drago had taken his share and then some, probably when they were packing Mama into the truck in Cambridge. No surprise that his asshole brother had taken off, leaving Georgi as their mother's sole nursemaid.

This was all he needed. The situation with Charleen was already shaky. She'd called him at midnight saying that his sister had been wheeled into a private room but that there was a cop guarding her door. Seeing that, Charleen had high-tailed it out of there and was now demanding to know what kind of trouble Rosica had gotten herself into. Little did she know that Georgi was in trouble too. On top of that, when she learned that Georgi's sick and unpleasant mother had moved in with him, it would be *Dovizhdane* Georgi. And, as long as Mama was sleeping in his dining room, he could forget about ever getting any other woman interested in him. *Dovizhdane* to company. *Dovizhdane* to sex. He'd be trapped in this dump, endlessly changing Mama's bedpans and listening to her constant complaints.

Georgi hesitated a moment, staring at the floor. Then his face cleared and he moved quickly to the living room. He grabbed a large fringed pillow from the sofa and headed back to Mama's room.

CHAPTER 56

Rosica tried to figure out what time it was. The window blinds were almost closed, but she could make out the pinkish-gray light of dawn. The room lights were dimmed, and there was a hushed early morning sound broken by occasional muted announcements over the fuzzy PA speakers. She needed to come up with a plan and she needed to make her move quickly.

If she could find her phone she could call Milo. Would he know her real identity by now? Too risky. She tried to reach the drawer of the bedside table but that involved twisting and it hurt too much. She saw a plastic spoon on top of the table, grabbed it and was able to drag the drawer knob forward. But peering inside, she found only a remote control for adjusting the bed and a laminated sheet of useless hospital phone numbers.

She raised the head of the bed, hoping that the mechanical sound wouldn't alert the cop outside her door. This elevated position made her head throb, so she took a sip of water and breathed deeply until the pressure eased off. From this new vantage point she could see out the window to a parking lot not far below. She was on the second floor. Her odds for escape had just improved.

The nurse hadn't mentioned any damage to her legs beyond bruising. Rosica rotated her ankles, then pedaled them back-and-forth. So far, so good. She swiveled them side-to-side and lifted each one several inches under the sheet. They felt intact, but weak. She would have to risk trying to walk.

Rosica sat up carefully and slowly swung her legs over the edge of the bed. Her head spun, but it cleared after a moment. Her ribcage ached and she definitely wanted more pills, but she needed to keep her mind as clear as possible.

She carefully placed one foot on the floor, testing it with some of her weight. Then she tried her other leg and stood up, holding on to the bed rail. A bit shaky, but OK. This might work.

Rosica shuffled into the bathroom and relieved herself. Then she splashed water on her face and studied herself in the mirror. She washed a bit of blood off of her cheek, but it was clear that her helmet had protected most of her head from the cuts and scrapes that covered her torso.

She searched the tiny room for her clothes and phone, but the closet was empty. Out the window she watched a lone car pulling out of a parking space. Directly below stood a row of bushes. She quietly raised the window sash. Thankfully, the hospital believed in fresh air and operable windows. She closed the sash, returned to bed, and pulled the sheet up over herself before pressing the call button strapped to the bed rail.

A long few minutes later a nurse, a different one from the night before, wheeled in a breakfast cart and positioned it over the bed. "Did you ring for something?"

"My rib hurts. May I please have more of that pain reliever?" Rosica asked.

The new nurse checked the doctor's notes in Rosica's chart, looked at her sideways, and disappeared.

Rosica eyed the food in front of her. *When was the last time she'd eaten?* She took a sip of the weak coffee, then a few bites of toast. She shoveled down some eggs, then pushed the cart out of her way.

By the time the nurse returned, Rosica was behind the door with her breakfast tray raised high. As the nurse saw the empty bed and started to look around the room, Rosica whacked her hard on the back of the head and watched as she crumpled to the floor.

Rosica stripped off the woman's scrubs and put them on in place of her hospital gown. A few moments later, the nurse let out a low moan, but by then, the window was open and Rosica was gone.

CHAPTER 57

Why did Milo suddenly need to meet her at the building site at the crack of dawn? Iris was barely awake when he'd called. Now she sat, bleary-eyed, on the restaurant's front steps, sipping coffee from a travel mug in an attempt to jump-start her brain.

She could hear the purr of Milo's motorcycle moments before she watched him pull into the driveway.

Milo parked, took off his helmet, and flicked his braid out from under his jacket. Iris could read exhaustion in his gray eyes.

He unlocked the front door and led them back to the kitchen. They sat on the two stools that Iris had brought over from her basement the week before.

Milo ran his thumbnail back and forth along the edge of the stainless steel counter.

"Is there a problem with the project?" Iris prompted.

He shook his head and took something out of his back jeans pocket. He unfolded the piece of print paper and slid it in front of her. "Guy in my band told me to check out the *Globe* website last night."

Iris recognized the photo of Rosica Bakalov taken from her

driver's license.

"This the woman who set you up, who's been harassing you?" he asked.

"Yeah. Why?"

He lifted his eyes and reluctantly met hers. "I've been seeing her for the last two months."

Iris' knuckles went white as she gripped her mug tighter.

"She said her name was Rose Baker and that she was a teacher. Guess I got played."

A few moments passed before Iris' brain could formulate a question. "Did she ever ask about me?"

"Sometimes your name would come up when she'd ask about my work." A bit of color rose on Milo's cheeks. "Like if I said you'd done a nice design detail, I noticed Rose would get pissy. I figured she was jealous of other women and I stopped mentioning you."

"Didn't you notice how much she looked like me?"

"She had different hair and eyes and a whole different vibe." Milo studied his thumbnail. "I did notice...once when she was sleeping...I realized who she reminded me of. But lots of people look alike."

As Iris focused on Milo's dark lashes, the image flashed into her head of him naked in bed with Rosica, the woman who looked so much like herself. She could see the snake tattoo running around his chiseled bicep and across his strong back. She instantly cleared the picture from her mind. "Have you told the police that you know her?"

"I wanted to talk to you first, make sure it was really her. The picture doesn't look that much like her now. The article says she's Bulgarian, but Rose didn't have an accent. She was a little crazy, though. At first it was good-crazy, but then she started getting clingy-crazy. I was ready to cool things down."

"The police found some marked bills from the robbery in the mother's house where her motorcycle was registered. It's her."

"She told me she was an orphan." Milo stared out the window. His voice cracked as he continued, "The *Globe* said she was in a bad accident on her bike. Is she dead?"

"No, I was told she made it out of surgery at Mount Auburn Hospital and she'll be OK. When's the last time you talked with her?"

"She called me maybe two days ago. She wanted to make plans for this weekend, but I blew her off." Milo dropped his head into his hands. "Oh, man. This can't be happening."

"Wait." Iris squinted a little. "You thought she was an orphan? Didn't you ever meet her mother or brothers when you went to her house?"

"Rose had her own place, an apartment near Central Square."

"I wonder if the police know about it. She might have rented it under the Rose Baker alias. There could be more evidence there, maybe the credit cards she took out in my name."

"I'd hate to rat her out to the cops, Iris. We had a thing going for awhile."

Iris placed her hand on top of his and looked into his eyes. "I know. But she's done some serious shit. What if we went to the apartment ourselves and looked around to see if there was anything the police needed to know about. Would that be OK?"

Milo made a defeated shrug. "Oh, God. I guess so."

"Do you know how we can get in?"

He looked embarrassed. "I have a key."

"Good. Let's check it out." Iris headed toward the front door, calling over her shoulder, "How should we get there?"

"I've got an extra helmet. Hop on my bike."

CHAPTER 58

Damn that nurse for having such small feet. Rosica felt blisters forming on both heels as she made her way through the back streets around Harvard Square, walking carefully past quiet houses, keeping an eye out for the cops. The sun was up and people were starting to leave for work or school, but no one in hospital-centric Cambridge seemed to pay any attention to the sight of an exhausted-looking woman in scrubs trudging home after a night shift.

The keys to her apartment, along with her clothes and wallet, had been taken away while she was in the hospital. Thank god nothing the police had confiscated could lead them to this address. Rosica circled her block before darting across the empty yard toward the rear of the apartment building. Her rib was throbbing in tandem with her feet but, as soon as she got inside, she'd be able to take the light blue Percocet tablets she'd found inside the nurse's pocket.

Rosica lifted a heavy rock she found by the chain-link fence, then gingerly climbed the fire escape to the second story kitchen window. One whack with the rock broke the glass near the inside window latch. She slid out the sharp shards, opened the latch, and quietly raised the sash. After climbing through, she kicked off the offending clogs and peeled off the scrubs.

Naked, Rosica retrieved a glass and poured herself some water. After she'd washed down the Percocet, she checked the contents of her refrigerator. She took out a container of leftover minced pork, sniffed it, then spread it on a piece of white bread. As she ate, she wandered around her three rooms, the "love nest."

This was the first place she'd been able to call her own. She'd had her first real boyfriend here. Dammit. A single tear tracked down her cheek.

Rosica was reminded of a boar hunt back in Romania where she'd been hired to pass trays of drinks to rich people on horseback. She remembered the sight, hours later, of the near-dead boar dragged back, a bleeding trophy cruelly lashed to a cart. There was a look of defeat in the animal's eyes and a frenzied, triumphant glee in the eyes of some of the hunters, their cheeks pink, their voices loud. She wondered if Iris Reid had a similar look as she'd chased Rosica into traffic and heard the crash of metal and glass.

But that bitch hadn't defeated her. Rosica was still alive and free and she'd reinvent herself again. She'd use Reid's money to build a new life, and then she'd find a new guy. To hell with Milo. He'd blown her off the last time they'd spoken. How dare he?

Had he ever cared about her? By now, did he know who she really was? Good, let him figure out how she'd fooled him. But would he tell the police about this place?

With that thought, Rosica decided to get dressed. After painfully slipping on a pair of ripped jeans, a *Pixies Rock* T-shirt, a baseball cap, and some high-top sneakers, she climbed up on a stool inside her closet to retrieve a backpack from the top shelf. In it she'd stashed a few thousand dollars and a semiautomatic Ruger pistol she'd bought at a gun show in New Hampshire. Mama still had Rosica's cut of the bank robbery proceeds. Had the cops gotten to Mama and Drago before they could escape with the money? They would have gone to Georgi's farm house. She'd have to call him as soon as she could get her hands on a burner phone.

From her bureau she took out a long brunette wig and added it to some spare clothes in the duffle bag. She threw in some toiletries from the bathroom and some credit cards and IDs that she'd hidden in a baggie in the toilet tank. Just as she was stuffing her laptop and its charger into the bag, she heard the unmistakable deep, choppy sound of a motorcycle in the street outside.

Was it Milo? She ran to the kitchen window and recognized his shape from a block away. But there was someone on the back of the bike, arms encircling his waist. She watched Milo park, then saw a woman dismount. She was wearing Milo's leather jacket. The woman unbuckled her helmet and shook out her hair.

Rosica couldn't believe her eyes.

CHAPTER 59

Iris gave the weatherbeaten three story clapboard building an appraising look. "Maybe this isn't such a good idea," she said as Milo slipped his key into the front door. "We should call the police."

He stopped, his hand on the knob. "But there may not be anything incriminating here. You'll see—it's pretty bare bones."

The day was starting to heat up and Iris slipped off the leather jacket that Milo had lent her for the ride over. "OK. We'll check it out."

He led them up a rickety staircase to a second door, unlocked it, then stepped aside to let her into a spartan living room. The shades were half down, so she turned on a table lamp and was surprised to see a sofa that was a knock-off of the Le Corbusier she had in her own house. There were some wilted flowers on a side table. Milo hung back in the doorway.

"Does she have a desk?" Iris asked.

Milo shoved his hands into the pockets of his jeans. "She mostly worked on her laptop at the coffee table."

"Why don't you search in here while I look in the bedroom.

See if you can find the laptop."

Milo remained in the entry. "I don't know if I can do this, Iris—look through her stuff."

Iris gave him an understanding nod. "Wait there then. I can do it."

He slid down the wall to sit on the floor. "Thanks."

A copy of *People* magazine sat splayed open, face down, on a modern-looking side table. Iris opened its only drawer, and lifted the sofa cushions. Finding nothing but lint, she moved on to the bathroom.

Discovering some rubber gloves under the sink, she slipped them on. The medicine cabinet held a lot of make-up and one bottle of pink pills with no prescription label. She lifted the heavy porcelain toilet cover to check inside the tank; she'd watched her share of police procedurals on TV. Nothing was hidden inside.

She moved on to the bedroom, finding lots of clothes jammed into the bureau and some flashy jewelry lying out on top, but no secret documents or credit cards hidden in the sock drawer. When Iris saw a large packet of condoms in the bedside table, she quickly slammed the drawer shut. She found nothing hidden under the mattress.

Moving on, she headed toward the closed closet door, then hesitated. If this were a mystery, a murderer would be hiding in there. "Milo, can you come here for a minute?"

With him at her side, she turned the knob and slowly opened it. Iris exhaled when she saw that the deep space held only clothes. But it looked like things had been dumped from their hangers onto the floor. A stool was overturned. Iris righted it and stepped up to check the top shelf. She lifted out a shoe box and looked inside. She showed Milo an empty bullet box. "Did you know that Rosica had a gun?"

"I'm beginning to think I didn't know anything about her." He left the bedroom shaking his head.

A minute later, Iris heard Milo yell, "Oh, shit. You need to see this." He stood in the kitchen facing a broken window. "Be careful." He held out an arm to stop her. "There's glass on the floor."

Iris fished out her phone. "Now it's time to call the police."

CHAPTER 60

Dressed in a hoodie and jeans and carrying a backpack, Rosica blended into the crowd streaming along Mass Ave toward Harvard Square. She slipped into a T-Mobile store to buy a burner phone, assuring the salesperson that, no, she wouldn't prefer the kind that connected to her T-Mobile account.

Rosica sat on the brick steps of the "Pit", the small sunken amphitheater that's considered the center of the Square, and adjusted the settings of her phone so they wouldn't reveal her location. She turned away from the man holding a sign offering a "free Bible quiz" and punched in the number for Georgi's cell phone. After several rings, she heard his truculent voice, "Yeah, who's this?"

"It's me. I just got out of the hospital. Tell me what's happened to Mama and Drago."

She heard labored breathing from the other end, then "How'd you get away? I heard they had a cop on your door."

Rosica looked around to make sure she couldn't be overheard. "I don't have much time. Tell me about Mama and Drago."

"Drago's taken off and Mama...didn't make it."

"What do you mean? She's dead?"

"What did you expect? You led the cops to her door. Drago and me tried to move her before they got there, but the stress was too much. I'm in the back yard now digging her grave."

"Oh god." A few moments passed in silence. "So you've got my money now?"

"Yeah, not that you deserve it after sending every cop in the state to look for us."

"Where did Drago go?"

"How am I supposed to know? The shithead took off this morning with his money and isn't answering his phone."

"I'm coming out there to get my share."

"You better make it fast. I'm not sticking around much longer. They've got our faces on the news."

"Hey—I'm not the one who shot the bank guard!" she hissed in a loud whisper, then pulled the rim of her baseball cap down. "You need to lie low. Give people time to get distracted by the next news story. Then you can slip away. I'll help you, but you need to stay there. I have to wait it out here in town. In a few days, when things cool down, I'll come out and we'll leave together, OK?"

"I'll think about it."

"Listen, little brother, if you leave with my money, I'll hunt you down and nail you to the wall by your balls. You know I'll do it."

"Fine, I'll wait. But don't take too long."

Rosica shoved the phone back into her jeans pocket. She sat for a minute trying to take in the news that her mother was dead. She would never show it in front of her brothers, but she felt desolate. Was it her fault? Mama had loomed over Rosica, larger than life, molding the daughter with her cleverness and her cynicism. Despite her nastiness, all those months of caring for the old woman had strengthened the bond between them. She wiped away tears.

"You OK?" asked an older woman sitting nearby gripping two garbage bags to her chest.

Rosica nodded, smiled weakly, and rose to her feet. She started walking up the avenue toward Porter Square, the direction of Milo's building site, knowing that this was a bad idea.

The sun was nearly overhead by the time she covered the eight blocks and stood across from the Victorian house, still under construction. She was too far away to see any signs of activity.

She crossed Mass Ave at the next corner. In the large plate-glass window of the drugstore, she caught sight of her reflection and headed inside to find a large pair of sunglasses. While there, she also purchased a bottle of water, some extra-strength ibuprofen, and a copy of the *Globe*, stuffing them into her backpack. She left and followed a side street to an alley that dead-ended at the site's back yard. As she followed a row of evergreens that ran along the edge of the property, she could hear saws and drills operating inside. The back kitchen door was propped open with a chair, allowing the sound of pounding rock music to spill out. She crept closer so she could see the driveway. There was a green pick-up and a small Japanese car, but no sign of Milo's two-wheeled ride.

It had been more than an hour since Rosica had watched him drive up to her apartment with Iris. Were they still there? What were they doing and were they doing it in her bed?

Rosica sat back on her haunches to assess the situation. As she'd told Georgi, she needed to hole up in Cambridge for a few days until the cops' attention moved on to someone else. She couldn't go back to her apartment and she couldn't risk trying to get to Georgi's farm house, forty minutes away.

She considered staying in the basement of the construction site before remembering that Milo had said a woman ran yoga classes down there at night.

Then, a smile slowly formed as she realized she knew of a perfect hiding place—an empty house nearby that was comfortable, had air conditioning, and probably even had cable TV still working. Iris Reid's house.

The revenge would be sweet.

CHAPTER 61

Rosica popped two ibuprofens and sipped her water as she trudged up the hill to Iris' house. The last time she'd been paying attention, Rosica had learned that her nemesis had moved full-time into the blond guy's place around the corner. She sincerely hoped that status had not changed. Of course, Reid's relationship with the blond guy hadn't stopped her from trying to put the moves on Milo.

There was a realtor's sign in the yard with a "For Rent" attachment swinging below the broker's name, and Rosica could see a lockbox attached to the front doorknob. She saw no one passing by within view so she mounted the steps and studied which of the numbered buttons on the device looked the most worn. She pressed them down in several combinations before the lock sprang open. Rosica let herself in and flipped the deadbolt shut behind her. She'd have to be on the alert—ready to hide or make a quick escape if a broker turned up to show the place.

The house's interior looked as impressive as when she'd peered in through the windows. She wandered from room to room admiring the classic furniture, a mixture of modern-looking stuff and a few antiques. Reid had probably gotten the fancy pieces from her family the same way she always seemed to get things handed to her.

The living room was painted the color of oatmeal and the office next to it was a dark, glossy blue. Rosica took out her phone and snapped some pictures so she could copy some of the design ideas when she got her own place.

She noticed a grouping of photos on the bookshelves in the office. In one of them, Reid was a girl, maybe twelve, sitting on the deck of a sailboat with an older couple and a boy with his arm around her, her family no doubt. She studied Reid's face, so like her own. How had she ended up with all the good stuff—two happy, rich parents and even a brother who seemed to care about her? Rosica remembered reading in the paper when Reid got picked up by the cops that the brother was her lawyer. *She* should have had that life instead of her own shitty one.

In the refrigerator she found a few cartons of yogurt, half a bottle of white wine, and some catsup on the door shelf. There was a package of coffee in the freezer, thank god. It took her awhile to figure out how to turn on and fill a coffee machine that looked complicated enough to fly a jet plane. The contraption began to thump and hiss, spit and whizz like a steam engine. She found a large mug in a cabinet and slid it under the nozzle just as the dark liquid gushed out.

Nursing the hot brew, she stared out the kitchen window at a nearby house with its tidy garden in back and several large trees. She would enjoy living in this neighborhood with its old houses and small landscaped yards. Obviously, she'd burned her bridges in Cambridge, but there must be other places like this in America. Not a big city, not the suburbs, but not the sticks either. While sipping her coffee, a reasonably-fresh yogurt waiting on the counter, she imagined that kind of life. This was where she *would* be living if life was fair.

Still, just this morning she'd been a prisoner, but now, a few hours later, she was making plans for a new life. She'd travelled clear across town and not a single cop had spotted her. She was a survivor and, if life hadn't dealt her a decent set of cards, she'd take some better cards away from someone who didn't deserve them.

Rosica spread out the *Globe* on the counter and flipped through the pages until she found the article about her on the front page of the metro section: ***Motorcycle Accident tied to Bank Robbery***.

There were photos of all four of them, even Mama, taken from their drivers' licenses from several years before. Rosica's didn't look much like her anymore. Still, she should disguise herself when she went out. She couldn't cut her hair much shorter, so she'd have to wear the wig. She was walking stiffly because of her rib injury, but that should heal in a week or so.

She'd also need a new wardrobe. She placed the mug inside

the dishwasher, out of view, and climbed upstairs to see if Reid had left behind any clothes. If the woman wanted to poke around *her* apartment, Rosica would return the favor. The master bedroom looked inviting with its oval window and round turret, as did the king-sized bed with its fluffy white duvet. She stretched out on top of the covers. She'd sleep a lot better tonight than she did last night, especially after she polished off the rest of that wine in the fridge.

In the walk-in closet were a lot of empty hangers where clothes had been removed, but there were still a lot of things left behind—cashmere sweaters in a rainbow of colors and dresses which looked far more expensive, if way more boring, than any that Rosica had ever owned. She checked a label and saw that Reid was one size larger than her, but Rosica could wear things blousy, cinched in with a belt. She pulled down an empty suitcase from a shelf in the closet and started tossing things inside. She added lacy bras and sexy underpants from the top drawer of a bureau to her collection. It seemed only fair that Reid would provide Rosica's going-away wardrobe.

CHAPTER 62

Iris got out of the passenger side of Ellie's Volvo and the two women walked the block from Ellie's house down to the Paradise Café. As they approached the door, Iris saw Luc reading a paper behind the mahogany coffee bar, his lips pursed in concentration.

At the bang of the screen door, his head jerked up and he rounded the bar to embrace Iris.

She had already filled him in on the morning's developments while waiting for Ellie to come pick her up at Rosica's apartment.

"That rocker-dude contractor, *my* contractor, was shacking up with the psycho?" Luc's voice was dark with anger. "And now she's escaped? How do we know they aren't in this together?"

"They aren't." Iris held Luc's arm as he led them to the last unoccupied table. "Rosica Bakalov played Milo to get information about me. He's incredibly embarrassed about it. The police are still grilling him."

"Why is this woman so obsessed with you?" The cords in Luc's neck reflected his anger.

Ellie slid into a blond Bentwood chair across the table from them. "This babe's gone way further than just scamming you.

265

When she was riffling through your computer stuff, she must have seen your resemblance to her, but from what you told me in the car coming over, it's like she now wants to *be* you."

"Milo said she'd get furious if he even mentioned my name. He'd been trying to break it off but was scared to piss her off."

The Café's long-time waitress, Louise, sauntered over and asked what she could bring them. She had a diamond stud in her nostril today instead of the customary gold ring and it twinkled in the sunlight. They ordered three espressos. Luc called after her,"And three slices of the lemon Ciambella."

Iris sat, staring without seeing out the window overlooking Mass Ave. "Rosica must have panicked when I started nosing around."

"You stirred up a hornet's nest," Ellie agreed.

Louise delivered cups and plates to their table.

Luc ripped open a packet of organic sugar and dumped the granules into his tiny coffee cup, his agitation palpable. "Where is she now? She could still be coming after you."

"That depends on whether getting revenge against me is a higher priority than getting out of town. Her picture's all over the news." Iris drank her espresso in one swallow, enjoying the warm rush of caffeine. She broke off a forkful of cake and closed her eyes. "I wish I could get inside this woman's head."

"Know any criminal shrinks?" Luc suggested.

Iris and Ellie locked eyes and both said, "Felicia!"

"Who?" Luc asked.

"Mack went to Med School with her and we've stayed friends," Ellie said. "Iris has met her."

"Won't she be in Truro on vacation now with all the other shrinks?"

"No, that's next month. They all go in August. I'll call and see if she can fit you in."

*　　　*　　　*

An hour later Felicia popped her head into the waiting room of a nondescript professional building in Watertown. She wore a roomy caftan and her frizzy hair hung loose down her back. She ushered Iris back to a cozy office featuring large upholstered furniture placed in a conversational U. Iris sank into a plush chair and filled her in on everything that had happened with Rosica.

Felicia took notes on a blue pad. At certain parts in Iris' story, her eyebrows rose, but she didn't interrupt. When Iris was finished, Felicia stared down at her lap as if making up her mind about something. After a few moments she said, "It's always difficult to diagnose someone without meeting them and talking in person, but I'll give you my impressions. I suspect that Rosica has BPD, borderline personality disorder, which is very hard to treat. Her impulsiveness, her sudden anger, her reckless behavior—those are some of the signs. A person with BPD sees things as black or white. It's like a switch gets flipped. Someone's either on her side or they're the enemy and must be crushed in order for her to survive. If her condition is escalating, she could potentially become violent."

Iris leaned forward. "Rosica strikes me as being cunning. Wouldn't her survival instincts focus her on escaping from danger? She was in police custody last night. Wouldn't she see the police as a greater threat than me?"

Felicia cocked her head. "A BPD person really only operates in the present, not the past or future. Given the fact that she chose to stay in this area after the bank robbery and to continue to harass you, she may view you two as connected. Even if one part of her perceives you as the enemy, another part may have blurred the boundaries between you. You're the person she might have been if she had had more opportunities."

CHAPTER 63

Rosica needed to search the house for a hiding place in case anyone invaded her space. First, she found the charger in her backpack and plugged her phone into an outlet in the kitchen. She'd start in the basement. Using a flashlight that she found in the front hall table, she headed down the narrow staircase. Two windows, too high up and too small to crawl through, allowed dim light into the unfinished underground space.

A huge stack of boxes lined one wall. They were carefully lined up with labels like "Christmas ornaments" and "Kitchen cookware." No surprise that Reid was the over-organized, anal type. Rosica noticed an alcove under the stairs that might serve her purpose, but she'd need a second exit away from the stairs so she wouldn't get trapped.

A door led into a second room where a bunch of mechanical things with pipes and wires coming out of them were located. The room was too clean for a basement. Would potential renters want to come down here to inspect this stuff? The husbands might, she guessed.

On the far side of the basement was a metal door. She

opened it and found steps leading up to angled steel double doors. She pushed a pole to lift the heavy door leaves, which let out a piercing squeal and then a noisy thud as the doors banged to the ground. Rosica was blinded by sudden bright light. She reached out for the door edges to close them and retreated, with her heart thudding, pulling them behind her. No silent escapes through the bulkhead.

As she backtracked through the basement toward the stairs, her flashlight picked out a table with an electric saw attached. She'd seen Drago use a chop saw like that during one of his short-lived stints as a carpenter. There was a big wooden object on top of the table and she moved closer to inspect it in brighter light. She ran the beam of her flashlight over its smooth surfaces and touched them with her fingertips. They felt even softer than they looked. She didn't know what the object was, but she knew it was beautiful. What had at first looked like a pillow-sized blob was actually a swoopy, undulating thing that belonged in nature. She inspected it from different angles, and its form was different from each vantage point. Rosica felt curiously drawn to it. It spoke to her in a way that she'd never experienced before. Maybe if she'd had a different life she would have been an artist and made sculptures like this.

Tucking the flashlight into the waist of her jeans, she wrapped her arms around the wood piece and lugged it up the rickety stairs to the first floor. She brought it into the kitchen and placed it on the counter. As she ran her hand over the surfaces, she became aware of the rumbling in her stomach. She was starving. The microwave clock in the kitchen read six o'clock. She'd eaten the yogurts and polished off the last of the wine hours earlier. She wouldn't be able to sneak out to get groceries at the Star Market in Porter Square until the middle of the night. According to earlier research on her phone, the store was eight blocks away and open 24/7. But, damn, she was hungry now. She searched the kitchen more thoroughly and found a can of tuna hiding behind a dozen spice jars in the small pantry. She located a can opener in a drawer but, at this point, she'd have been willing to use a rock to pry it open. She shoveled down the oily flakes with her fingers, only stopping after she'd carefully licked every last bit of oil.

It would soon get dark and she still needed to find a safe spot to hide in the rambling house. Her sore rib was aching again and she needed to rest. She made another circuit of the first floor, from kitchen to dining room, to living room, to office. There were several closets she could fit inside, but a real estate broker was likely to open them to show a prospective renter. It made more sense for her to hide on the second floor closer to a bed and a TV. It would give her more time to get to her hiding spot after hearing the front door opening.

Rosica liked the idea of sleeping in Reid's big bed, but the master bedroom faced the road and, even with the curtains closed, a bedside light might be visible from the street. She eliminated the adjoining guest room, also facing the street. But, on the far side of the central staircase she discovered a small room tucked away from prying eyes. A sofa and TV took up half of the room, and a bookcase filled with catalogs and plastic bins lined the side wall. She could see that the bins held samples of wallpaper, fabric, and tile. This must be overflow from Reid's office downstairs. Rosica could entertain herself going through these boxes to help her decide how to decorate her next house. It would be like having her own HGTV show.

She peeked out through heavy lined curtains to see if any of the neighbors' windows overlooked this spot. Several did. But she also saw that a section of the first floor kitchen jutted out below, its roof an easy jump away. It would be a perfect escape route, but only after dark.

Rosica padded off to collect her phone from the kitchen and popped down several more pain pills. Once she'd retrieved her backpack from under the master bed, she returned to Reid's study. She laid out her toothbrush and her loaded Ruger side by side on a table next to the sofa, then settled in to binge-watch her favorite reality TV shows.

CHAPTER 64

The next afternoon, Iris sat in front of her laptop at her makeshift desk in Luc's living room, staring at luscious images of de Gournay wallpaper. She had an inspiration about having the facing side walls of the dining spaces papered with whimsical tree designs, not in a fuddy-duddy all-over wallpaper look—just one wall per room to give the spaces some depth. She could match the background color with the Venetian plaster pigment on the adjacent walls and the two rooms could be done in complementary colors. She had already had Milo frame archways into the hall between the two rooms. But maybe the accent wallpaper should just be on one wall instead of two. Wasn't de Gournay paper breathtakingly expensive?

She scrolled through different patterns when *the Tree of Life* design caught her eye. It looked familiar. Didn't she have a sample of this from the Boston Design Center back in her own office? She could pin it up on the actual wall to demonstrate the effect for Luc.

Iris' cell phone buzzed.

"Good news." Sterling sounded chipper. "The DA's office is dropping the case against you. Once Rosica was caught they could

273

see the resemblance between you two, and how she could have staged the rental agency tape. They also found a few of the marked bills from the bank robbery in her mother's house, so the case against you fell apart."

Iris' end of the phone call was silent.

"Iris, did you hear what I said?"

"I'm processing." The Sword of Damocles hanging over her head for the last four months, the nightmare she had been living, it was now gone. Pouf. "Hang on a minute."

Iris headed for Luc's freezer. She took out a bottle of vodka, unscrewed the cap and took several long swigs. She placed the bottle on the island counter and sank onto a stool. "OK, I'm back..."

"But we can't forget that crazy Rosica is still on the loose," Sterling continued. "I've arranged for Greg Peretti to come stay with you until she's captured."

"Hold on—what do you mean 'stay with me'? You mean sleep here with us in Luc's one-bedroom condo?"

"Until Bakalov is caught, she's still a threat. She no doubt blames you for the accident that got her captured. And the police don't have enough resources to help you. They can only do something *after* you're attacked."

"That's so reassuring."

"Greg does this all the time for our clients who need

protection. You won't even know he's around."

"You don't think anyone will notice a strange guy following me around at the construction site?"

"Better than the alternative, Sis. He can't get there 'til two. Lie low until then. He'll fill you in on the protocol."

"Fine. I hear and obey."

Before turning off her phone, she checked the time. One o'clock. She had an hour before Greg-the-bodyguard would turn up—just enough time to take Sheba for a walk.

CHAPTER 65

"Walkies!" Iris called out. Sheba roused herself from sleep faster than a Tesla could reach cruising speed. Iris snapped on her leash and they strolled the two blocks back to their old familiar driveway so they could drive the Jeep the two miles to Fresh Pond.

"I need to run inside to get something. Want to wait in the car or come inside?" Sheba's enthusiastic look suggested that she wanted to stick with her mistress.

Iris inserted her key and swung the front door open. "You miss our old house, don't you, girl?"

The Basset hound ran into the kitchen, nails clattering on the hardwood floor. Iris carried the mail in from the vestibule and stood at the kitchen counter flipping through ads and flyers that hadn't been forwarded before dumping them all into the recycling bin. Sheba raced around in circles, sniffing the floor eagerly, then streaked by Iris up the stairs.

A minute later Iris heard a thud, like a heavy book being slammed on a table, followed by a loud canine yelp of pain. She flew up the stairs and punched open the door to her study.

Rosica Bakalov was lifting a window sash, one foot resting on the sill. Iris stared at her, struck once again by the eerie sensation of looking at her own face.

She turned to see Sheba curled into a ball in a corner whimpering. Iris stepped toward her dog just as Rosica shouted, "Don't move." Rosica pulled a gun from the waistband of her jeans, and pointed it at Iris' chest.

Iris froze.

Rosica lowered the gun and climbed stiffly back into the room. "So, I finally meet my twin. It looks like the best woman won."

Iris stole a quick glace at Sheba. The dog was panting, her eyes pleading with her mistress to help her.

"Good dog," Iris said under her breath.

"You know," Rosica said, looking over her shoulder out the window, "this actually isn't a good time for me to go outside. I think I'll wait until it gets dark. Besides, after ruining all my plans I don't think you deserve a quick death."

Rosica's last word booted Iris' synapses into high gear. "Wait—the police are looking for you. I can help you escape. You can hide in my car while I drive you out of the area. But here's the deal—we drop my dog off at the Vet on the way out of town."

"Tempting offer." Rosica's free hand was wrapped around her torso, clutching her ribs. "Maybe you *can* be of some use. But forget about the dog. Turn around and I'll follow you to the car."

"You look like you're hurting. Let me get you some aspirin." Iris took a tiny step closer to Rosica.

"Stay back and turn around."

Iris turned slowly, signaling Sheba with her eyes that she would get help. If she could only get close enough to Rosica she could use a karate move to disarm her.

Iris heard her dog whine softly just as the back of her head seemed to explode. She saw white flashes and felt like she was falling, falling backward. Then, everything faded to black.

IRIS

CHAPTER 66

When Iris came to, the first thing she felt was her head burning with pain. She could see only inky blackness. She blinked, but could still see nothing. Panic rose in her throat.

She tried moving her arms. She could wiggle her fingers but her arms were pinned to her sides. They weren't tied together but when she explored around her with her fingers she felt some kind of frame. A cage? Her legs were stretched out straight. The air was hot and stifling.

Her heart hammered, pumping adrenaline into her veins. She began to hyperventilate. Her worst nightmare. She was buried alive!

Just as she was getting light-headed, she heard Hannah's sing-songy voice in the back of her mind saying, "Take a long cleansing breath and clear your mind. Breathe in through your nose and out through your mouth. Breathe in, deeply. Now breathe out slowly. In....out..." She tried to follow the yogini's instructions to calm herself. After a few long minutes she was able to think again.

Could she hear anything? Birds? Yes, there were birds singing somewhere nearby. Was she outside? Probably not. Rosica wouldn't risk having anyone see her drag a body out of the house.

She smelled the faint aroma of cat urine—the odor of old-fashioned insulation batts.

Iris moved her head slightly to the right, then to the left. On the right there seemed to be some space, but on the left her nose bumped into a hard surface. Overhead there appeared to be slanted wood joists. She tried lifting her hands and confirmed that there was a little space to move on the right side, but her left hand was wedged in. So, this space was triangular-shaped. Suddenly, she got it. She'd been stuffed into the tiny storage space under a roof eave, probably the eave alongside her upstairs study.

Sheba—was Sheba OK? She shouted the dog's name. After a few moments she heard a weak whimper. She shouted again, "Good dog. It's going to be OK. WAIT." Sheba knew that last command. She had to help her dog.

Conserve your oxygen. Think—how had Rosica gotten her in here? She didn't remember ever seeing an access door in her study, but maybe it'd been behind the sofa left there from when her parents had owned the house. That heavy old thing was one of the few pieces of furniture that Iris had never moved. Shit, Rosica was strong. With the fingertips of her right hand, she felt through the stud framework along the side wall for a door or break in the plaster. When she felt nothing, she slipped off her espadrille and felt along the wall with her bare right foot. She felt a slit. She ran her big toe up as far as she could reach, only a few inches, but the slit seemed to continue. She awkwardly managed to get her foot back into the shoe and tried to kick out at the panel but she couldn't get enough strength behind it. She tried to shift her weight to allow her leg a longer backswing, but the space was too confined. Rosica must have stuffed her in here head first, then pushed the sofa back in front of the access door to block it as an exit. That would explain why her nose and left cheek felt like they were full of splinters. She screamed in frustration and heard another whimper from Sheba.

"It's OK, Sheba. I'm going to get us out of here. Then we're going to move in to the new house with Luc and the three of us will be a family. And you'll get lots of treats, and walkies, and steak every night." Iris tried to keep herself from crying. "And I'll get my life together, I promise."

But first, she needed to get herself out of this crawlspace. If she couldn't break through the side walls, there was only one other logical choice. She felt the surface under her. Since it was an old nineteenth century house, the rough floors were covered with boards, not plywood. Some nails in a board under her right hip must have popped out because one board was higher than its neighbor. Iris dug her fingertips into the raised end and was able to lift it an inch. She kept wiggling it until she ripped off a piece about two feet long. Once that slot was opened up, she found that she could use the broken wood as a pry bar to lift up more sections.

It was slow work because of the confined space and she had to twist herself sideways with her back up against the inside wall. At some point in the last fifty years an owner had added fluffy pink insulation between the supports and it itched against her skin. She kicked it into a pile at her feet in order to reach a section of floor boards wider than her hips. These joists, set sixteen inches apart, were the bones of the house. Once she had the area from her hips to her knees opened up, exposing the lath-and-plaster ceiling of the living room below, she slid as far as possible to one end, hitting her sore head against the end wall in the process, until her feet were positioned between the joists directly over the plaster. She kicked down with her heels until she felt the lath crumbling. A nasty cloud of horsehair plaster dust had her coughing.

Once she was able to breathe again, she inched herself toward the hole she'd made, angling her hips slightly while letting her legs dangle through to the room below. With a final call to Sheba, assuring her that she was going for help, Iris held on to the ceiling joists and lowered herself a few feet into the room, letting herself fall the remaining six feet to the carpet below. She heard an ominous crack from the leg she landed on and excruciating pain shot through her body. She tried to catch her breath while listening for any sign of Rosica. Her eyes landed on a small white device that still remained on her living room étagere, and she called out, "Alexa—call 911!"

The efficient mechanical voice answered, "Dialing 9-1-1."

A dispatcher asked what her emergency was.

Iris gasped out her address. "Rosica Bakalov, the bank robber, attacked me." She added, "Bakalov has a gun... my dog's hurt."

Hurried footsteps sounded on the stairs. Rosica appeared in the doorway, a suitcase in one hand and her other arm wrapped around Iris' wood sculpture.

She glared at Iris, eyes narrowing. "You are such a pain in the ass! It's your turn to suffer."

Sirens could be heard in the distance.

Rosica vanished through the kitchen.

CHAPTER 67

The back door slammed shut, and Iris curled up on the floor to wait, calling feebly up to Sheba, "Hang on, girl!"

She heard the sirens getting louder, then, moments later, pounding on her front door. Iris tried to crawl toward it but only got several feet before she collapsed. She could hear their loud hammering.

I need help for Sheba and the cops can't get through that heavy door unless I open it. She dragged herself closer to the entry by her elbows. In a final burst of determination, she lifted herself far enough onto one hip to turn the lock. The door sprang open.

Iris rolled out of the path of several police officers rushing in. She croaked out, "Bakalov ran out the back door."

The lead cop issued commands into a microphone on his shoulder while Iris grabbed the ankle of another officer who was carefully holstering her gun. "My dog's hurt. Upstairs in study— left rear. Bakalov kicked her. Needs Angell Animal Hospital."

Soon, EMTs were strapping Iris to a gurney, but she kept repeating, "Help my dog!" before she passed out.

* * *

Hours later, Iris could see harsh light through the crusty slits of her eyes. She felt something bulky and rigid encasing her leg and saw Luc hunched over in a chair by her hospital bed, quietly watching her face. He looked drawn and worried.

She reached over to touch his arm and saw relief flood his features.

"You're awake. Are you OK? Are you in pain?"

She tried to smile as he dragged his chair closer. "I've been better."

"I should never have left you alone with Bakalov still on the loose."

"No, I should have waited for the bodyguard Sterling sent before I went out." Then Iris remembered. "Sheba—how is she?"

"Ellie's with her at Angell." Luc choked up when he said, "She's got a ruptured spleen. They're operating on her now."

"But she'll be OK—right?"

"The vet thinks so. Ellie's been texting me with developments."

Iris' hands clenched into angry fists. "Did the police get that bitch? I'll kill her!"

"Not if I can get to her first. She took your car and got

away." Luc lowered the metal rail on the side of the bed.

"What are you doing?"

"Slide over." He climbed up onto the bed beside her and wrapped his arm gently around her.

After a few minutes Iris murmured sleepily, "How badly am I messed up?"

"Broken leg—a fractured fibula they called it, but it's a clean break. A bunch of bruises too. The cast can come off in a few weeks."

"Perfect."

"This time, Bakalov's gonna get locked up for good," Luc murmured.

As Iris drifted off, she remembered Rosica's words: *It was Iris' turn to suffer.*

CHAPTER 68

Two days later, Luc rolled Sheba into the condo on a veterinarian's dolly. Ellie followed carrying Sheba's favorite toy kitty, the one with most of the stuffing gone and one eye missing.

Iris swung her cast-heavy leg off the living room sofa, wincing at the weight and the dull pain as she wobbled over to the entryway, kneeling awkwardly beside Sheba. "How's my good girl?" She buried her face in the dog's fur. It had been agony waiting for the animal hospital to agree to release her. Iris had Skyped a visit with her dog on Ellie's I-pad, but it was still a shock to see Sheba's abdomen wrapped in bandages. The dog raised woebegone eyes to her mistress.

"The bad lady's all gone. It's gonna be OK now." Iris couldn't rub Sheba's belly so she wrapped her arms around the dog in a gentle hug. After a few moments and a few tears, Iris looked up at Ellie. "Thanks for staying with her. Did the vet say anything else?"

"She came through the operation fine with no infection or bleeding. They gave me some pills for you to hide in her food if she seems in pain. Mack is going to stop by tonight to check her vital signs."

Iris couldn't help but smile. Ellie's husband was a pediatrician. "I'll bet this is the first time he'll use his skills on a dog."

Ellie leaned down to scratch Sheba under the chin. "She's not just *any* dog."

"I was going to grill her a steak tonight," Luc said unhappily, holding up the sheet of paper he'd been reading. "But her aftercare instructions say she needs to go easy on rich food for a few days."

Sheba shot him an even more miserable look.

"Don't worry, girl. I'll think of something else tasty to make." Luc lifted the stocky Bassett Hound and gently set her down on the sofa, then turned to Iris. "Now you get back on that couch with your leg raised like the doctor ordered. Both of you are *my* patients now."

Iris muttered "Yes, Nurse Ratched," as her cell phone buzzed. The caller ID announced Lieutenant Choi.

Luc and Ellie waited expectantly while Iris said "I see" several times through pursed lips, then, "That's a small relief. I liked that sculpture." Iris ended the call and pounded her fist on the coffee table. "They found my Jeep at the long-term parking lot at Logan Airport. No Rosica. That monster's managed to escape again!"

"Let's just hope she's flown back to Bulgaria," Ellie said.

CHAPTER 69

Rosica hated having to leave the sculpture behind, but she wanted to ditch Reid's car at the airport to muddy her path with the cops. She left it seat-belted in the passenger seat of the Jeep. Even without a fractured rib, there was no way she could carry the large, cumbersome piece on public transportation, and the last thing she needed was to attract attention.

From Logan Airport, she took the free Silverline bus to South Station, then a half hour ride on the Commuter Rail out to Abington, all the while keeping her hair tucked up in her baseball cap and avoiding eye contact with the other passengers. She walked the long mile from the train station to Georgi's farm house to avoid any chatty cab or Uber drivers who might remember her. By the time she trudged up the dirt driveway, she was in a foul mood. Her sore rib ached and the sight of her brother sitting in a rusty metal chair in the back yard smoking a joint did nothing to improve it.

Georgi was in his mid-twenties. His washed-out coloring, scraggly mullet, and weak chin, made him look like a man with few prospects. Rosica and her older brother, Drago, had gotten all the looks and smarts in the family. Mama had frequently reminded Georgi that he had been a mistake in every sense of the word, and he seemed to have settled into the part.

"Come help me with my suitcase," Rosica called, dropping it on the patchy lawn.

Georgi scowled at her. "Carry it yourself. Are the cops on your tail this time?"

She gestured behind her at the empty driveway.

"You're not moving in here, I'll tell you that much."

"I came for my money, not your company. I need to lie low for a few days, then I'm out of your life forever."

Georgi reluctantly extinguished the joint against the heel of his boot and placed it carefully on the arm of the chair. He led her onto the sagging porch. Rosica hadn't remembered the place being this run-down.

The porch door opened directly into a dark kitchen that made their East Cambridge one look like a spread in a glossy magazine. Pots and pans were piled up in the sink. Buzzing flies circled an open can of soup, and fruit flies hovered near a bowl of overripe peaches. A window fan vibrated like a helicopter taking off.

Georgi swept his arm vaguely toward the mess and muttered, "Maybe you can make yourself useful while you're here."

At the far end of the room a heavy purple curtain was strung on a pole across a large opening.

"You can sleep in Mama's room," Georgi said pointing with his head toward the curtain, then he froze as if remembering something.

Long seconds passed as Rosica's eyes drilled into her younger brother's downturned profile. "You told me Mama died before she ever got here...from the stress of having to run away... because of me."

"She did," Georgi sputtered. "She did. I still had to get a room ready for her, didn't I?"

Rosica considered pointing out the illogic of his having had time to prepare anything after Mama's panicked call on hearing the news of Rosica's accident on her police scanner. But she let the subject drop. Her choices for a safe place to stay were limited.

She shuddered at the sight of the dirty, rumpled sheets and lumpy pillows lying on the mattress set directly on the floor. Had Georgi, and possibly Drago, decided that the sick old lady was too much trouble to have around? Was this where her mother had died?

"You have a washing machine? These are filthy."

"In the basement."

After tossing sheets, pillowcases, and towels in the washer, Rosica retreated to her new room. She opened the suitcase and sat on the bare mattress, lifting out some of Reid's delicate lingerie and a silky dress. She stroked the soft fabrics, even smelled one of the cashmere sweaters. It had that "rich girl" smell—a tiny bit of perfume and a definite lack of sweat.

She lay back against the wall and closed her eyes, remembering the pristine white duvet on Reid's big bed. She thought of the immaculate kitchen with its sleek marble counters and fancy coffee machine, the high ceilings and soothing paint colors. She could go for a cup of that strong coffee right now.

The pathetic thing was, Georgi didn't even realize that his place was a dump. He belonged here living among his clutter and unwashed dishes, smoking dope. But Rosica didn't. In fact, she could see now that she'd never belonged in the life she'd been dealt. Even the "love nest" was too modest. Rosica was smart and worked hard. She deserved more.

She belonged in that photograph in Reid's living room, on a sailboat surrounded by elegant parents and a handsome, adoring brother. *She* belonged in that house on Washington Avenue with its sculptures and paintings.

She lay down on the mattress. She could so clearly imagine the face of the woman who had gotten the life that Rosica should have had. A face so like her own. *It wasn't fair.*

CHAPTER 70

The next day, when Georgi drove his truck off to God-knows-where, probably to score more dope, Rosica decided to search the house for the money. She didn't want to argue with Georgi about how much of it was hers. Since Mama would no longer need her share, there was extra to be divided up. Drago had taken off, so he'd forfeited his claim. Mama had paid off the mortgage on the East Cambridge house before they had to abandon it, so that investment was a loss. Then, Mama had parceled out Georgi's money to him, partly to get rid of him because he got on her nerves, and partly so he could buy a house as a go-to-ground resource for the family.

Nevertheless, Georgi would have to bail on this house too before going deeper into hiding, so half of the money from the bank robbery had already been wasted.

Rosica quickly found the satin pillowcase of cash in the second place she looked: the freezer. Her brother was so stupid. She scraped off the ice coating the pouch, opened the frozen drawstrings, then spread the bills out on the kitchen table. It took her twenty minutes to stack them into piles and count them twice.

There was only around $240K left, so Drago had no doubt taken more than his share. Rosica counted out $220K and stuffed it in a compartment of her new suitcase, sliding the pouch with the remaining money back in the freezer behind a stack of upright Hungry Man TV dinners. She'd leave Georgi a little money to start his new life or else he'd be sure to come after her.

She was wearing one of Iris' gauzy cotton dresses with long flared sleeves. She tied a scarf around her hair and donned the large sunglasses she'd bought a few days before when she'd stopped in that drug store before going to hide at the Washington Avenue house.

As she retraced her steps back to Cambridge on the Commuter Rail, Rosica worked out her plan. She'd switch to the Red Line subway and stop in Central Square to buy a short mousy brown wig. She'd find a room in an Airbnb near the blond guy's condo where Reid was staying. The Porter Square area was a convenient spot for visitors, right by the subway stop. Maybe she'd even score a place close enough to see into the condo's windows.

She'd need to buy a serious telescope or binoculars, maybe with night vision. She bet that the gift shop at the Museum of Science sold them. She'd passed the place many times on her motorcycle while cruising into Boston. She felt a pang when she remembered her sweet old Honda and how Reid had chased her under the wheels of an SUV, demolishing her ride and almost killing her.

Rosica sat back in the hard train seat, closed her eyes and half-smiled. She'd taken the most important step of her plan the night before. She'd navigated onto one of her favorite forums on the encrypted dark web and requested help in fulfilling a fantasy.

Iris Reid was in for a big surprise.

CHAPTER 71

The next morning around eleven o'clock, Iris and Luc were hit with a blanket of moist heat as they exited the condo. It felt more like a sultry morning in Louisiana than New England.

"Oof. Let me get the car," Luc offered.

"It's only a few blocks. Plus, I need to get used to these crutches." Iris regretted that commitment as she arrived a few minutes later at the building site, glistening with sweat, her wrists and armpits aching. Luc had to carry her up the tall porch steps.

In the two front dining rooms, workers on stilts pirouetted precariously around each other while vigorously plastering the high ceilings, OSHA safety regulations notwithstanding. Paint samples were taped to various walls.

Iris and Luc followed the loud rock music and general construction noise to the rear of the building where Milo and his two finish carpenters were carefully installing the kitchen cabinets. Milo glanced up, then dropped his gaze quickly, resuming his work.

Luc walked around the space, back and forth, swiveling between the lower cabinets, as if he were moving hot pans and plates from counter to counter.

Milo finished fastening a base cabinet, then set down his power screwdriver to rub his hands on the back of his jeans. He ran an eye over Iris' cast and crutches. "Sorry about the accident. You OK?"

It was no accident. "I will be."

Luc spent a conspicuous moment staring at Milo. A current of guilt, suspicion, and blame swirled around the room.

Iris smiled at the contractor. "When you get a chance, can we go over the deliveries—which items are already on site and which ones we're still waiting for? We don't want any of the fixtures or furniture to be stuck on a slow boat from Italy."

"Sure thing," Milo said. "Will you be here for awhile? I'd like to finish getting these cabinets in first. The stainless steel fabricators are coming at noon to template the counters."

Luc leaned down to speak privately to Iris. "I need to get over to the restaurant. Do you want to stay here? Will you be able to get home OK?"

She made a dismissive gesture. "Get going. You need to earn as much money as you can to pay for this renovation. I can take my time hobbling back."

Milo called out, "I'll see she gets home."

Luc said over his shoulder to Milo as he left the room, "Place looks good."

Iris made her way to the staircase, propped her crutches

against the wall, and sat a few steps up on a tread to make a list of remaining tasks on her phone. Once she had finished, she called her rep at the de Gournay showcase at the Design Center and offered her a pair of complimentary dinners at the new restaurant in exchange for expediting the wallpaper order from England. It was a relief that everything seemed to be on schedule considering that the new restaurant needed to be open and ready for business in a month's time. Iris and Luc's personal renovation upstairs would have to wait until the restaurant space was finished. Milo's crew would continue to work on the living space during the daytime hours when the restaurant would be closed.

She made her way awkwardly up the staircase on her rear end to check the boxes of delicate glassware and china plates that Milo had stored out of the way on the second floor. Amazingly, nothing appeared to be broken, so far.

Downstairs, the doorbell rang, but there was no way that Iris could get to the door in time. She heard the squeak of the heavy front door opening. They really needed to oil those hinges. She added another note to the list.

Milo called up to her, "Looks like some lights just got delivered from some manufacturer in Italy."

By the time Iris butt-bumped her way down the stairs, Milo had opened one of the three large boxes and was examining an elegant cast bronze arm, holding an electrified torch. "Excellent workmanship," he said approvingly.

"The sconces, finally! I'd better check them all to make sure none are damaged." Iris lowered herself gingerly onto the floor and Milo handed her a utility knife before he returned to the adjacent room to continue hanging the arched mahogany and glass doors on the enormous built-in hutch.

After Iris finished checking the first box, she moved on to the next. An envelope with her handwritten name was taped to the top. Maybe Rupert, the antiques dealer, had included a personal note. She tore it open, smiling, then felt a chill envelop her as she read *Reid:1. Bakalov:1. Game on.*

CHAPTER 72

Milo pried Iris' phone from her violently shaking hands so he could call Lieutenant Choi. As they waited for the detective to arrive, he sat on the floor with his arm awkwardly around Iris. "It's going to be all right. She can't get you," he soothed. "Now that the police know she's still nearby, they can find her."

Iris gave him a grim smile. "They didn't catch her last time. She only had a five minute head start, with cops on the way, and she still managed to escape."

Lieutenant Choi entered the restaurant followed by two other officers who immediately began to search the building, nervous hands hovering near their holstered guns. Choi squatted down to face Iris. "I understand that this is distressing for you, Ms. Reid, but it actually provides a good lead for tracking Bakalov down. I have officers searching the neighborhood. Can you show me the note, please?"

Iris appreciated the change in Lieutenant Choi's manner now that she was a victim instead of a suspect. She pointed to the piece of thick card stock lying on the floor where she'd dropped it next to its envelope.

"How many people have handled these?" Choi looked pointedly at Milo.

"Only me," Iris said. "Milo read it but didn't touch it."

Choi put on a pair of purple nitrile gloves and transferred both items into separate clear plastic evidence bags. "We need to figure out when Ms. Bakalov could have gotten access to that box. We got hold of the UPS driver and he doesn't remember any envelopes taped to the boxes when he scanned the bar codes." Choi rose gracefully to her feet. Milo helped Iris stand and balance on her crutches.

"Can you think of any way that Bakalov could have known that these boxes were being delivered today?" Choi asked.

"We've had lots of deliveries every day for the last few weeks," Iris said. "She could have sneaked up and attached the envelope to any one of them or even shoved it though the mail slot. The UPS guy just drops stuff on the porch and doesn't even bother ringing the doorbell anymore."

Milo looked up sharply. "But he did today. The doorbell rang while I was carrying some doors up from the basement. I propped them against the wall in the next room, then went to the front door in case they needed a signature."

"Was the UPS guy there?"

"No, just the boxes. I didn't even see the truck leaving."

Choi started taking notes on her phone. "How many minutes

was it between the bell ringing and you opening the door?"

"A few."

Choi shoved her phone back into her pocket and hurried to the entry door. Iris followed on her crutches. By the time Iris arrived on the front porch, Choi was in the side yard studying the dirt near a large evergreen tree.

"I think I've found a woman's sneaker footprint," Choi announced.

"Does that mean that Rosica was out there waiting and watching me open the door?" Milo sounded nervous.

"Probably." Choi kneeled down and peered closely at something on the ground. "There's something else here."

Iris called out, "What is it?"

Choi straightened up, holding what she'd just stored in an evidence bag. "How strange. It looks like a dog biscuit."

CHAPTER 73

An hour later Iris sat perched on a stool in the safety of the condo's kitchen, washing and arranging a head of butter lettuce in a bowl.

"I still think you should stay with my friends in Rome until she's caught," Luc said as he expertly chopped red onions, avocados, and crabmeat to add to their salad.

Sheba sat at Luc's feet, big Bassett Hound eyes gazing up hopefully for some falling morsels. The low-slung dog had put on extra pounds in the last few days from all the convalescent treats she'd been scoring.

"And who's going to make sure all the finishing touches come together for your fancy new restaurant?"

"Your life is more important than the restaurant!"

"Sterling is sending over Greg Perelli to act as a bodyguard for Sheba and me. After that dog biscuit threat, I'm not letting Sheba out of my sight."

Luc poured some vinaigrette from a cruet into a small ceramic bowl and whisked in a few spoonfuls of mayonnaise. "I don't want to let either of you out of *my* sight either. Maybe I should take some time off, or maybe you should come hang out with me in the *Paradise* kitchen."

Iris limped up behind him and wrapped her arms around his waist.

He twisted around and kissed her. "What would I do if anything happened to you?"

"Don't worry. I'm not going to let Rosica hurt either Sheba or me again."

They carried plates and bowls to the table and started eating. Awhile later the sound of the doorbell interrupted their post-lunch espressos.

Luc ambled to the entry door with Iris limping behind him. A mild-mannered-looking man stepped into the vestibule as Sheba approached, growling suspiciously.

"Oh," slipped out of Iris' mouth when she saw her new protector. She had met Greg the one time, months before, in Sterling's office, but had forgotten how unprepossessing the guy was. He was the same height as Iris' five foot-eight inches, wiry in build with bland looks that would make him hard to pick out of a line-up of middle-aged businessmen. But his shrewd brown eyes looked like they missed nothing. He carried a small suitcase with a sleeping bag bungee corded onto it which he dropped on the floor. He looked inquisitively at Iris and Luc, with a side glance at the softly growling Bassett Hound.

Greg smiled at Iris. "I find it's helpful to look underwhelming in my business."

Luc regarded Greg skeptically, "Are you packing?"

Greg lifted the flap of his sports jacket to provide a glimpse of a holster, then wandered into the kitchen, Luc and Iris trailing him. He walked over to each of the three windows and looked out, studying the surrounding buildings. "Gotta landline?"

When Luc gestured toward the wall phone, Greg unscrewed the transmitter on the handset and squinted inside. "No bugs here but I'll do a complete search of the whole place after we talk. You got one of those Alexas or other listening devices?"

"No way. They creep me out," Luc answered.

Greg nodded. "Me too." He made his way back to the living room and perched on one of the two upholstered chairs. Iris and Luc sat opposite him on the sofa while Sheba sniffed Greg's tie-up leather shoes.

"Nice dog. Shame what Bakalov did." Greg rubbed Sheba between her ears. "Your brother filled me in on the threat, Ms. Reid. I've checked out the security on this building and it's actually pretty decent. The weak spot is the basement, lots of ways to break in through the windows or doors, despite the security cameras down there. So, the best line of defense is for me to stay close to you until Bakalov is caught."

"Are we talking about 24/7 surveillance?" Iris asked. "Where will you sleep? This is a one-bedroom condo."

"That a pull-out couch?"

Iris and Luc looked at the sofa and simultaneously shook their heads.

"No problem. That's why I brought my bedroll. I'm used to it."

"Don't we need another guard to keep watch while you're sleeping?"

"Nah," Greg said. "Ms. Bakalov will have to get through me to get to you, and I'm a very light sleeper."

* * *

Mid-afternoon, after Luc left for the restaurant, Greg announced that he would take Sheba out for a walk around the building instead of her leisurely sniff-and-stroll at Fresh Pond. He insisted that Iris keep her cell phone line open during his absence, even though he'd be keeping the building in view the entire time,.

Once Greg and Sheba went outside, Iris dutifully called Greg on her cell phone, then left it sitting on the living room table while she called Sterling from the kitchen landline. "What do you know about this guy?" she asked him in a hushed voice. "He doesn't look very tough."

Sterling chuckled. Her brother was the only man Iris knew

who chuckled. "Don't underestimate him. He was an Army Ranger. This guy has three tours of Afghanistan under his belt. He's worked for my firm for two years. Everyone swears by him."

"Am I paying him by the hour? It's going to cost a fortune and we don't know how long this will last."

"Don't worry about that." Sterling said. "I'll get my firm to work something out. Think of him as a wall between you and Bakalov."

Iris heard a key in the lock, so she ended her call and hobbled back to the living room. Sheba glared at Iris with her bloodshot Basset eyes; her abbreviated walk was no match for Fresh Pond.

"Mission accomplished," Greg announced, holding up a full poop bag.

This same dog-walking operation was repeated again later that afternoon while Iris tried to oversee the construction site remotely via phone calls to Milo.

Iris made hamburgers and corn-on-the-cob for dinner, then spent an awkward evening in the living room with Greg. He removed his holster after dinner and placed it on top of the neat pile of clothes in the corner next to his suitcase; he kept the gun itself on a side table within arm's reach. He settled in to read a Tom Clancy paperback while Iris caught up on e-mail, her laptop propped on the sofa arm, her leg on an ottoman.

The man had an annoying habit of licking his finger before turning pages while he read. Iris attempted to tune out the sight and sound of it. Finally, to get him to stop, she asked, "Do you have a family, Greg? Where do you live?"

He cocked his head. "I doubt I could do this job if I had a family. I have to be able to move around, spend nights here and there. It's hard to even find time for friendships."

"Why do you do it?" Iris asked.

"It's exciting." Greg's eyes lit up. "I get to use my skills. I get to help people. Every day is different."

Iris regarded him. "It sounds lonely. Don't you want to have a relationship?"

"It's a trade-off. I could never work a desk job." Greg shrugged and turned back to his book.

She excused herself soon afterward, went to the bedroom, and got ready for bed about an hour before her usual time. But several hours later, she was startled awake by Luc's shouts from the living room.

"Greg, it's just me! I live here." Luc called out.

Iris limped to the living room just in time to see Greg putting his gun back on the floor next to his bedroll. "Cool, man. Just making sure," Greg said before lying back down.

When Luc got into bed beside Iris he asked, "Is it safe— having this trigger-happy guy here? He almost shot me."

The next morning, grunting noises coming from the living room woke Iris while the sky was still dark. She looked at the lit-up hands on her bedside clock: five a.m. She shook Luc lightly by the shoulder. "Do you hear something?"

Luc bolted upright. "Huh? What is it? You OK?"

Iris whispered "I think it's Greg. Listen. What's he doing out there?"

Luc swung his legs out of bed and padded naked to the door to peer through the crack. "Jeez—the guy's doing one-handed push-ups." He turned back to Iris. "FYI: he's not as wimpy as we thought. He has quite the six-pack."

Iris groaned, "It's like we're living in a college dorm. I'll call Choi in the morning and make sure she calls us the minute she captures Bakalov."

"Nothing like having a miniature Rambo as your dorm parent."

CHAPTER 74

What *had she done?* She'd jeopardized the whole plan, writing that self-indulgent taunt just to jerk Reid's chain. And going into the neighborhood pharmacy to get dog biscuits. Did she *want* to get caught? Rosica nervously swallowed another bite of Pad Thai, take-out from the busy restaurant across the street.

Still, it had been too much, seeing that Reid had merely broken a leg. She'd stuffed her into the crawl space to suffer a slow, agonizing death while listening to her dog whimpering in pain. Then, watching Reid's doting boyfriend carry her up the stairs of Milo's construction site had made her want to vomit. That bitch always ended up getting men to take her side. Rosica didn't even *have* a boyfriend anymore, thanks to Reid's turning Milo against her. She had to laugh though at her inspiration to leave the dog biscuit behind as a threat to hurt the dog again. Reid had really wigged out at seeing that. Why do Americans care so much about their pets? But the sight of Milo comforting Reid afterward had negated Rosica's one small victory. Still, the game wasn't over.

She sat on her comfortable bed in the Airbnb's one room studio finishing her dinner. Writing that note had led to two unfortunate results. The cops now knew she was back in the area, and that made it risky to do much surveillance other than spying through her new telescope set up in the west-facing window. Amazingly, she'd found a fourth floor walk up in a big brick apartment building only a block away from Reid's condo, so now she could get glimpses into the front windows of the condo's kitchen and living room. The owner had left her a key in an envelope taped to the mail boxes and asked Rosica to water her plants.

The second problem was that Reid had hired a bodyguard. The guy didn't look too intimidating but, by the bulges under his jacket, he was packing. True, Rosica wouldn't be the one taking him on, but she needed to ensure a successful attack. If she could get her intel right, the bodyguard could be avoided entirely.

She needed to figure out his schedule. He'd spent the previous night there, unless he'd slipped out through the basement and returned in the morning the same way. But she'd noticed a light on in the living room in the early morning and had seen him walking around shirtless, so he was probably camping out there. Reid had stayed in the kitchen for most of the day, reading and working on her laptop, while the bodyguard had stayed in the living room. The boyfriend had come and gone. The only time that Rosica saw the bodyguard leave the condo was when he walked the dog. She was keeping a log of these walks. He'd made two twenty-minute trips today, at eight o'clock and at two, each time patrolling around the large condo building, studying basement windows and scanning the windows of adjacent buildings. During his rounds, she'd been careful to close her curtains, watching him through a small opening. He might take the dog out for a third walk after dinner. If he stuck to a regular schedule, and this guy seemed like the type who would, she could plan around his timing. Twenty minutes would be long enough for her accomplices to get in, long enough for what she had in store for Reid.

Rosica collected the debris from her meal and tied it up in a garbage bag. Then she opened her laptop and clicked on her special TOR browser to get into the dark web. She typed a series of commands until she reached the forum she was looking for and created a new heading: I've been a bad girl.

CHAPTER 75

Ellie came by the condo on Day 3. Greg buzzed her in and they carefully sized each other up before the women retreated to the kitchen. A well-bandaged Sheba waddled along after them.

Ellie whispered, "That's him? I was hoping for Kevin Cosner."

"Luc says he makes a better impression with his shirt off."

Ellie flapped her hands. "I'm not going there."

"Whatever. This protective custody business is making me crazy."

"Better than the alternative. How's the leg?" Ellie reached down to scratch behind Sheba's ears. "Are you two resting?"

Iris regarded her dog, whose eyes were closed with pleasure at Ellie's touch. "One of us is. The other is limping around this condo like a caged animal."

"You're supposed to keep your leg elevated. You're a terrible patient." Ellie reached into her purse. "I brought you something that will cheer you up."

"Drugs?"

Ellie rolled her eyes. She tossed the Metro section of the

Globe onto the kitchen table.

On the front page Iris noticed an artist's rendering of a building that looked vaguely familiar. "Oh, my god. What have they done to my design?"

"Read the critique," Ellie instructed. "It's written by Ezra Stein, the Globe's architectural critic. The one who hates everything."

Harvard's Graduate School of Design, in a bit of irony, is proposing to erect a totally banal guesthouse for visiting faculty on a highly visible site in Harvard Square. Vernon Elliott, a Cambridge architect, submitted the above design to the Cambridge Historical Commission last night to heated protests from a group of concerned citizens. The commission sent Harvard's architect back to the drawing board.

Iris snorted. "Poetic justice. I almost feel sorry for old Vernon, ass that he is. Speaking of architecture, I'm dying to see what's going on at the restaurant. The painters are applying a special, highly pigmented wash over the venetian plaster today. It's a technique I've been experimenting with, and I hope they haven't screwed it up."

"Do you want me to stop by and report back? I'd love to see

how everything's progressing."

"That would be great. Take lots of photos with your phone, OK?"

After Ellie left, Iris tried to get herself interested in the biography of Maria Callas she'd just started. But after ten minutes she began to feel stir-crazy again. She had goosebumps from the frigid central air-conditioning and wanted nothing more than to be outside, feeling the hot sun on her face. She finally laid her book down and went into the living room.

"I need to go out, Greg. Can't I wear a disguise and slip out through the basement? Maybe I could dress up like a man or something."

Across the room, Greg didn't even look up from the laptop he had set up as his temporary office. "Too dangerous. We don't know where Bakalov is. I've researched all the empty buildings with sight lines of the condo, but the subject hasn't been spotted yet."

"The subject," Iris muttered under her breath. "What am I? The object?"

Greg offered her a sympathetic look. "It's hard, staying under wraps like this when you're not used to it." He went back to tapping on his keyboard.

Iris drifted over to the window and stared out. "Should I be worried that the keys to Luc's condo were on the key ring that Bakalov took when she stole my car keys?"

Greg looked up at her sharply. "Were they labelled?"

"No. And between my house, the car, the new restaurant and Luc's condo, there werc almost a dozen keys there."

Greg rose and joined her at the window. "I don't like the idea of her having any opportunity for access. She's resourceful and motivated." He thought for a minute. "We can't change the entry key since that would affect all the other tenants, but I want to redo this unit's deadbolt. I noticed a lock store across the street on the next block. I'll pick up a new cylinder when I take the dog out at two."

CHAPTER 76

Rosica wound a hijab around her head and slipped on a tunic and pants before venturing over to the condo building to test which key from Reid's keychain would open the entry door. Ten minutes later, she'd just located the correct key, the heavy brass one, when a large ominous shadow loomed up behind her and she dropped the whole ring on the brick landing. Her heart skipped a beat but she then saw a man retrieve it and open the door for her. She mumbled, "Thanks, I think I left something in my car," and darted away. She trotted to the nearby lock store to get the key duplicated. On her walk back to the apartment, she passed two uniformed policemen. She hurried back to her building with her head down and eyes averted.

When she got to her room, breathing heavily, she shed her disguise. Her armpits were sticky with perspiration. She took a long shower, letting the pulse of hot water soothe her healing rib. She felt better after changing into one of Reid's silk teddies with a nice pair of matching briefs.

She retrieved her laptop, another burner phone, and a bag of Cheese Puffs from her suitcase and propped herself up on the bed. She stuffed a handful of the fluorescent orange bites into her mouth and activated the phone. It was a shame to sacrifice another one just to use for a hot spot, but she didn't dare tether her laptop into a nearby unsecured Wi-Fi signal. The IP address could expose her location. She'd better limit her session and buy a few more phones tomorrow.

Rosica onion-routed her way into the Tor browser and navigated to the dark web site. She clicked onto the forum and scanned for her code name: *Goldilocks*. There were already five responses:

Honey Bear: I can help you out, make it as rough as you can take it. Give me the time and place and I'll bring my equipment.

Big Bear: I know how to punish bad girls. Send details. You better not be a cop!

Biggest Bear: Sounds like someone needs a spanking. I'm your man.

Naughty Bear: Can't wait to discipline you with my steel rod.

Sadist Bear: I'm your fantasy and your nightmare!

Tough choice. Definitely the last two. But *Big Bear* versus *Biggest Bear*?

She asked all five of them to contact her at the e-mail address she'd set up for this purpose. After she'd chosen three of them for the task, she'd give them the time, place and where to find the key.

Then again, maybe she'd better fill them in on the group aspect first in case they wanted to weed themselves out. In her experience, men didn't hesitate if the group was multiple women with one man, but a several-men-with-one-woman scenario took a guy with a certain temperament.

CHAPTER 77

Iris had to admit that she felt safer since Greg had installed the new deadbolt cylinder. Watching the confident way he worked on it made her feel like she was in good hands. Even though she had a brown belt in karate, she knew she was no match for Rosica's gun. Still, Iris wished she could go to the dojo to get in a butt-kicking sparring session. But, of course, even if she could go out, she couldn't spar with her leg in a cast.

The restaurant would be closed tomorrow, Monday, so Luc would be able to keep her company then. Maybe they'd spend the whole day in bed with the bedroom door locked. That made her smile. Luc needed some relaxation. He'd been so worried lately about finances, with all the checks he'd been writing to pay for the renovation and start-up. A lot was riding on the new place gaining traction, quickly.

Why hadn't Greg or the police spotted that damn Rosica by now? Maybe she'd done the sensible thing and gotten out of town, out of the country even. Then Iris could have her life back.

Iris looked up to see Greg standing in the kitchen doorway. She checked her watch. Yup, three minutes before two o'clock.

He regarded the sleeping dog at Iris' feet. "Sheba, time for a walk."

Sheba opened her eyes, saw Greg holding her leash, and closed them again.

Greg walked over, clipped the leash to her collar, and made a clicking noise, as if to a horse.

Iris leaned over and tugged on her collar and Sheba finally got to her feet, casting Iris a long-suffering look as she waddled out of the room.

Iris locked the deadbolt behind them. She went to the coffee table to turn on her cell phone, scrolling to Greg on her contacts list.

But before she pressed the speed-dial, the doorbell rang and she dropped the phone.

She unlocked the door. "Did you forget a ..."

A tidal wave of large bodies pushed her back. Beer bellies and aggressive leers. Grabbing at her. A man with a scraggly beard yanked at her t-shirt. Ripped it at the neck before she could pull away. One with a pockmarked face tugged on her shorts zipper.

A third man shoved the top of a chair under the entry door's knob.

She was trapped! Her heart pounded explosions inside her body. She looked around, frantic for anything she could use as a weapon.

"Bend her over that sofa. The husband will be back soon," Beard yelled.

No—this would NOT happen! Iris let out a roar, spun sideways into Beard with a slashing elbow to the nose. He howled.

She pivoted again. Kneed Acne in the groin with her cast-free leg. His eyes mushroomed out of his face.

Chair guy grinned up at her, arms out. She felt his hot breath. Saw his bloodshot eyes. She blocked him with an inside-out forearm, bent his thumb backward. He doubled over. With stiffened fingers, palms up, she stabbed him in the eyes. He fell to his knees groaning.

"Want to play rough?" Beard charged her. Iris shoved his head down and kneed him sharply in his already-bloodied nose. She heard a crack. He slumped to the floor with a loud "ugh".

Where the hell was Greg? And damn this cast.

Acne rose up, and just like that he was on her. He held her arms behind her back with one hand and started unbuckling his belt. "You know you want this."

She kicked sideways on his knee with her good leg, jerked her hands loose and hammer-fisted him in the throat. He pitched forward. She thrust out her cast. He tripped over it and fell like a tree.

"GET...OUT!" Iris screamed. Slick with sweat, she tried to scramble toward the bathroom. She almost fell, grabbed onto the side of the sofa, and righted herself. She hurtled ahead, dragging her cast, until she threw herself inside. She tried to close the door, but fingers appeared curled around the edge. She put all her weight behind it and slammed the door hard. The fingers disappeared and she locked herself in.

Iris slid down onto the cool tiled floor. Her hands were quaking. Tears dripped onto her palms. She wiped her eyes with the back of her hands. *It wouldn't take long for these three to break down the door.*

She started shivering. Her elbow and knee throbbed with pain, but she forced herself to her feet. She found a large pair of hair-trimming scissors in the medicine cabinet. She waited behind the door clutching them in her hand.

She put her ear up to the wood. She could just make out their voices coming from the living room.

"Goldilocks broke my fingers!"

"She change her mind or was this a set-up?"

"Something's screwed up. We gotta get out of here before the husband gets back."

Iris heard some crashing, then silence. She sank back to the floor in relief and waited.

A few minutes later she heard Greg yell: "Iris, where are you?"

She reached the knob and opened the door but was too exhausted to get up. "In here."

CHAPTER 78

Iris blew her nose, wiped her tears, and looked up at Greg's concerned face.

"What happened? The front door was wide open."

Wearily, Iris told him. Greg swore and ran to the stairwell. A few moments later, he returned and grabbed the phone from his jacket pocket. "I'm calling Choi."

While Greg made his call, Iris staggered into the living room. *How could it look so undisturbed?* A side chair had been smashed and a smeared red handprint stood out against the tan linen sofa, but the rest of the room looked like it always did. Sheba sniffed the blood stain. "Stay away from that, Sheba. It's part of a crime scene."

Iris sank into a chair and phoned Luc. "I was just attacked by three guys in the condo."

It took Luc all of five minutes to get there. The first thing he did after entering was to grab Greg by his jacket lapels. "You were supposed to protect her," Luc said between clenched teeth.

Greg shoved Luc away and glared at him.

Iris hobbled over and took Luc's hand. "It wasn't Greg's fault.

The guys timed their break-in for while he was out with Sheba. We think they were waiting in the stairwell until he took the elevator down. The police are on their way and Greg's trying to get the security tapes."

"But what happened? Are you OK?" Luc was pale.

"I'm OK now." Iris and Luc sat down on chairs, avoiding the blood-stained sofa.

"'Who were these guys?" Luc asked.

"I overheard them talking. They seemed to think that I had arranged their break-in, then changed my mind. They referred to me as Goldilocks. I don't know...it was so confusing."

"Fucking-A!" Luc reached over and seized her hand in a warm grip. "Bakalov must have put them up to this. How did you manage to fight them off? Your leg's in a cast."

"They weren't experienced fighters. Just a bunch of horny, middle-aged jerks. I roughed them up, then locked myself in the bathroom until Greg returned. But they got away before Greg could catch them."

Luc looked at Greg standing by the entry door. "How did they get in here? Wasn't the deadbolt just changed?"

Heat rushed to Iris' cheeks. "I opened it. I thought it was

Greg coming back for something."

"Iris!"

"I wasn't thinking. It all happened so fast."

"This woman's got to be found and locked up now! The three asshole guys too." Luc glared at Greg. "You've been here how long—four days? Why haven't you found out where she's hiding? It's got to be someplace around here."

"We've been looking. The woman's a con artist. She blends into the woodwork. It's not easy tracking down someone like that."

"Look harder! Iris was almost gang-raped because of this low-life!" Luc retreated into the kitchen and returned with a package of frozen peas. He handed it to Iris. "Put this on your bruised knee, babe."

The entryway intercom buzzed. Greg got up. "Who is it?"

"Milo. I've got some invoices to drop off for Luc." Greg looked to Luc for his OK and buzzed him in.

Luc stood up and started to pace. "Where is Choi? She's sure taking her time."

"She was out on some other case. Said she'd be here as soon as possible," Greg turned to check his phone for messages. He looked carefully at the door as it opened.

When Milo entered, he glanced around at the three of them: Luc and Greg glowering, Iris in a torn t-shirt holding frozen peas against her knee, and a smashed chair on the floor. "This a bad time?"

The men shouted, "No," while Iris said, "Yes."

Milo looked around uncertainly and handed Luc a pile of papers. "These suppliers and subs need checks as soon as possible, so I figured I'd drop them off with Iris. I didn't know you'd be here." He turned to Iris."The paint washes in the front rooms look amazing. I brought you some pictures." He fished his phone out of his jeans pocket.

"We're a little preoccupied now. Three guys tried to attack me while Greg was outside with the dog. We think that Rosica sent them. Thank god I know karate but they got away. We're trying to track down the men and Rosica while the trail is fresh."

"Holy shit. You fought off three guys with your leg in a cast?" Milo's eyes shone with disbelief, then admiration.

From the other side of the room Greg approached him. "Have you been in touch with Bakalov? Do you know where she's hiding?"

"Hell, no. Get out of my face, man."

Greg stiffened, skeptical.

Iris moved to the window, looking out. "For Rosica to know Greg's schedule—the only times when he wasn't inside with me—she must be able to see or hear inside this condo. Greg's already checked for bugs." Iris squinted at the buildings across the street. "I think she's staying somewhere with a view of our windows so she can watch us."

The three men joined her, crowding all together at the large window.

Greg said, "I've gone over all the properties around here. There's a guest house several blocks away, but the owners say they have no single women staying there at the moment. The rest of the places are a church, a museum, private apartments, or commercial buildings with no short-term occupants. The police have been patrolling the neighborhood as well."

Iris pointed to a large brick structure a block away. "What about that building there?"

"It's apartments. All the tenants have leases." Greg said. "There've been no new tenants moving in in the last few days."

"Ever heard of Airbnb?" Iris asked, shading her eyes. "I see a glint of something. Fourth floor window, second window in from the corner. See it?"

Just as they all fixed their eyes on the window, its curtains snapped shut.

Greg headed for the door. "I'll check it out."

Milo said, "I'm coming with you."

"No. Stay here. You're a civilian. She's dangerous."

"There's probably a back door so there should be two of us. Besides, I'll recognize her."

Greg quickly strapped on his holster, slipped in his gun, and threw on a jacket to conceal it. "Fine. Luc, you stay here with Iris. Bakalov might circle back here if she sees us leaving."

CHAPTER 79

Rosica watched the condo's living room through the telescope in disbelief. Un-frigging-belivable! Three macho dudes from the dark web couldn't take on one middle-aged woman with a cast on her leg?

She had fully expected those lugs to leave a traumatized Reid behind. Whether they made a clean exit or not didn't really matter since they couldn't lead the cops back to her.

Still, the message was sent: Rosica could toy with Reid whenever and wherever she chose, and not even a bodyguard could protect her.

But that message had gotten messed up. Reid had protected herself. She'd won again!

It would take the cops days or even weeks to follow her digital footprints to the dark web dudes or the fake e-mail account or, eventually, to the burner phone which she'd already destroyed. Still, it was time to move on. She'd head out to the the airport on the subway and catch a plane to Miami. She'd use what was left from Reid's savings account and her share from the bank robbery to get herself a nice townhouse, maybe overlooking the water, with a palm tree or two.

Rosica moved efficiently around the studio, tossing clothes and supplies into Reid's elegant suitcase. When she got to the beautiful brass telescope, wondering if packing it in her carryon might attract undue attention from the TSA at the airport, she sighted through it for a parting look into Reid's happy world.

Shit—Milo was there. Reid had her three men around her, no doubt providing all sorts of comfort. Milo looked so fine in tight black jeans with his strong tatted arms and cool braid down to his ass. They'd still be together if it wasn't for that woman.

Reid was looking out the window. Her shirt was torn but she didn't look very messed up. Wait—she was looking out at the buildings. The men were coming over to join her.

Rosica backed away from the window and threw the last few things into her bag. She slipped on a tunic and pants and wrapped the hijab around her head.

Taking one last look around, she saw the western sun glinting on the telescope in the window. She grabbed it, tossed it on the bed, and tugged the curtains closed behind her.

She hurried down the staircase to the basement and cautiously opened the back door into the alleyway. She followed it to a side street, then forced herself to slow down and saunter across it in no particular hurry. Glancing left in the direction of Mass Ave, she froze and almost dropped her suitcase when she saw Reid's bodyguard jogging toward the apartment's front entry with Milo close behind. She pulled the hijab over the side of her face facing them.

Could Milo recognize her in this disguise? Rosica didn't dare head their way but she needed to get to the subway on Mass Ave, four long blocks away. She ambled up a driveway, then, when she was out of sight, ran through two back yards, over a fence and out to the next side street.

She took a quick look behind her but didn't see any pursuers so she slowed down and cut over to Mass Ave. She was now across from Reid's condo but didn't dare check to see if anyone was watching her from its windows. She hoped that Reid wouldn't recognize her own suitcase being carried by an apparently Islamic woman. She picked up her pace. The modern glass pavilion serving as the Porter Square subway entrance was still two blocks ahead.

As she approached it, Rosica tried to blend in with a crowd of giggling Japanese teenagers who came pouring out of the Porter Exchange building with its celebrated noodle shops. She could see the large red windmill sculpture spinning up ahead in front of the subway entrance.

She heard someone running and turned to see Milo half a block behind her in full pursuit. Their eyes met. Clutching the suitcase to her chest, she set off sprinting. She pushed through the subway station doors and leapt onto the escalator that descended three stories to the ticket booths. She squeezed by along the left side, half leaping, half running past the stationary people lined up on the right. Even mid-afternoon, the station was crowded. She could judge Milo's progress from the sound of angry cries from people being shoved aside. She didn't have a Charlie Card to get her through the turnstiles to ride the next four-story escalator down to the subway platform, so she would have to lose him somehow on that small intermediate level.

She took two steps off the escalator, then felt herself being tackled to the hard, concrete floor. She wriggled under Milo's grasp, shouting, "Help! He's trying to kill me!"

A group of bystanders quickly circled them.

"Let her up," one woman shouted.

"Take your hands off her," said a young man, trying to pry off Milo's grip on Rosica.

A transit cop approached. "What's going on here?"

"She's wanted by the Cambridge Police," Milo wheezed, scrambling to his feet while pulling Rosica up by the arm. "Call Lieutenant Choi. She's been looking for this woman for months."

Most of the crowd backed away as their protectiveness of Rosica evaporated.

"That's not true." Rosica protested. "He's my ex-husband and he's been stalking me."

Milo shot her an outraged look.

Greg leapt off the escalator and grabbed Rosica's other arm. He flipped open a license to show the transit cop, "I'm a P.I. We've been looking for this woman. She's wanted big-time by the police."

Just then, the pulsing wail of police sirens infiltrated the deep concrete structure. In a few minutes, Lieutenant Choi and several uniformed officers descended to join the group. Choi herself lost no time in pulling Rosica's hands behind her back and cuffing her.

CHAPTER 80

A week following Rosica's arrest, Iris went back to the hospital to have her cast removed. She felt a giddy sense of freedom.

She met Milo at the restaurant and they focused on pulling together the final details of the design. Mixing the landscape wallpaper scenes with the paint washes in the two dining spaces looked just as she'd envisioned. The large built-in cabinet with glass-fronted doors and the neoclassical fireplace worked well as focal points for each room. Iris was pleased to see that the bronze wall sconces added a bit of whimsy and cast just the right amount of flattering light. She was nervous when the long mahogany bar was brought over from the now-shuttered Paradise Café, worried about how it would fit where the old staircase had been, but it ended up looking custom-made for the space.

As the workers carried down the tables which had been stored on the second floor and set them in place, Milo caught Iris slowly rotating around, grinning as she took in the whole effect.

"Like what you see?" he asked.

She nodded. "I think we aced this."

"We're a good team." He gave her a long hug, then vanished

up the stairs.

Iris stared at his retreating back, mouth open.

Luc was otherwise occupied in the new kitchen, fine-tuning recipes with Arnold and Allegra. He raved about cooking on his fancy new range. He worked non-stop, and filled the walk-in refrigerators with white plastic vats of pickled watermelon rind with star anise, fermented pineapple hot sauce, and other exotic garnishes that could be prepared ahead of time. He even had the carpenters and Iris sample and then vote on the various desserts turned out by his new pastry chef.

* * *

It was opening night, a sultry Saturday in the second week of September with the summer's heat still radiating up from the concrete sidewalks.

Ellie and Mack stopped by the condo to pick up Iris in time for their nine o'clock reservation. Iris was wearing an emerald-green strapless Armani sheath bought specially for the occasion.

"You look like Audrey Hepburn in that dress," Ellie said approvingly.

Mack looked her up and down and whistled. "You clean up good, kid."

They approached the restaurant as dusk was deepening. Tiny

lights lining the circular driveway twinkled as they meandered up to the now-elegant Victorian structure, a sharp contrast to the dilapidated haunted house of seven months earlier.

Iris' group took their place in line behind half a dozen excited patrons as everyone made their way to the Maitre d' stand. A blond hostess in a black cocktail dress with her hair in a french twist managed the flow of diners to their tables.

Ellie bobbed her chin toward the hostess and whispered, "Isn't that...?"

Iris looked closer and her eyes narrowed. "Yoga Girl?"

They advanced to the front of the line where Iris said, "Hannah, I didn't realize you were working here."

Yoga Girl flashed them a huge smile. "Isn't it great? With the restaurant open at night, I switched all my classes to the daytime and applied for the job." She looked around. "I'd better show you to your table; it's a madhouse here tonight. Luc picked a spot in front of the fireplace for you."

Iris and Ellie exchanged a pair of sharply arched eyebrows en route.

After they were seated, Mack changed the subject. "Ahem. Will the *Globe's* food critic be here?"

"Luc thinks so." Iris scanned the room. "See that woman with the huge gold earrings who our friend Hannah is leading to a table by the window; I think that's her—Evelyn Lobel. No one's supposed to know what she looks like, and she uses a fake name for her reservations, but every chef in town knows exactly who she is. She comes alone and orders three entrees."

Ellie looked around the room. "This interior is positively poetic. I feel like there's a narrative behind it."

Iris beamed.

"And check out this menu," Mack added. "Charred octopus with roasted Japanese cauliflower, spiced yogurt and pumpkin hummus? How does Luc think up this stuff, and how are we supposed to narrow down our choices?"

"He's been like a mad scientist all summer, fiddling with combinations. We've definitely been eating well."

Louise, their favorite waitress from the old café, appeared at their table. "Do you believe the buzz in here? Can I bring you some drinks?"

For the first time in a long time, Iris realized that she was actually hungry.

"An *Autumn Daiquiri* for me," Ellie looked up from the cocktails menu.

Iris laughed when she saw a *Sheba Special* listed. "I doubt that my dog likes tequila, lime, orange and fennel, but I'll order it in her honor."

Mack went for a simple glass of Valpolicello, then leaned in to ask Iris, "What's happening with the Bakalov case?"

"When it comes to trial, probably next Spring, I'll have to testify. At least that's what Sterling says. Even Bakalov's shrewd lawyer couldn't get her out on bail, given how successfully she's escaped custody before. The vice cops recognized one of my attackers from the condo security tape and they brought him in, but he was communicating with a woman he thought was me on an anonymous dark-web sex site. I doubt that they can link that woman to Rosica. And, of course, she's trying to pin the bank robbery on her brothers, saying they forced her into helping them. Choi arrested the younger brother, the one who actually shot the bank guard, but the older brother got away and the mother, apparently, died. Rosica will be charged with attempted homicide against me as well as stalking, breaking and entering, etcetera. And they've linked her to other credit card and ID frauds in the area."

"Let's not forget what that bitch did to Sheba," Ellie added, taking a sip of the drink Louise had just handed to her and giving a thumbs up.

They gave Louise their appetizer and entrée orders.

"Do you think Bakalov's lawyer will go for an insanity plea?" Mack asked.

Iris considered this for a moment. Rosica almost certainly had a mental disorder, but was it enough to score her a get-out-of-jail card? "I'll bet she'll try that angle along with anything else she can think of. If she can convince some shrinks that she's insane, then, in a couple of years, she can convince them that they've cured her and she should go free."

Ellie shuddered. "I hope they lock her up and throw away the key."

Iris raised her glass. "Here's to Rosica Bakalov never crossing our paths again."

She observed the diners around them. At least one person at every table was photographing their plate. Iris peeked over at Evelyn Lobel. As predicted, the woman had three appetizers in front of her. She was slowly chewing, scrutinizing her food with the unblinking gaze of an alert owl.

Louise set out their first courses: fluke in braised seaweed for Iris, oysters with pineapple hot sauce for Mac, and cucumber soup with crab for Ellie.

"Wait—before you take a bite let me take a picture of these to send to Raven," Ellie took out her phone. Her painter daughter would appreciate Luc's artistry in plating his dishes, although Luc always made fun of other chefs who made tortured tableaus with tweezers and a swoosh bottle.

Iris wondered how things were going back in the kitchen. With so much riding on Luc getting all the details perfect, it was a wonder he hadn't had a nervous breakdown.

"I can't believe this soup. It's divine. Has Luc made this for you at home?" Ellie asked Iris.

"He spent an entire week adjusting the spices and add-ins. Are there peas in this version?"

"Yes, tiny, delicate peas. He must have great sources for his produce."

"Here, honey, taste this." Mack handed an oyster-filled fork to Ellie. "Dip it in this pineapple sauce."

"Whoa, it's spicy. What an amazing combination!" Ellie turned to Iris. "Your guy is a genius with food."

Iris felt her shoulders unbunch. *This money pit that she'd talked Luc into buying was going to be a success.*

They continued to share their appetizers, and the entrées after that. Between the pork belly with fennel and garlic; the scallops with squash, pistachio and saffron; and the wagyu beef with fig sauce and peanuts, none of them could choose a favorite. Each dish burst with its own overlapping layers of flavor.

Iris kept glancing casually over at Evelyn Lobel, and it looked like the woman was practically moaning with pleasure. She was photographing every exquisite morsel.

After the three of them polished off a Calvados caramel semifreddo and a brown butter apple cake, Ellie rested her elbows on the table. She leaned her chin on her fist. "I saw that the For Rent sign on your house was changed to For Sale. So, you're going to get rid of the old place after all?"

Iris smoothed her napkin on her lap. "It's time to move on.

Luc and I will stay in his condo until our apartment is ready upstairs. Then we'll move into the new place together."

At that point, Iris noticed a buzz in the air and looked up to see Luc threading his way toward their table. He must have changed clothes before coming out because his chef's jacket looked spotless and blindingly white. Iris could see pride in his eyes. She began to clap her hands quietly.

People at nearby tables joined the clapping. Soon everyone was standing up, giving Luc a standing ovation.

The exhausted chef looked taken back, but put his hand over his heart and, looking directly at Iris, took a slow, deep bow.

ACKNOWLEDGMENTS

Grateful thanks to my writing group for their encouragement and wise advice. To Dan Tenney, my motorcycle expert, for his patience in reading all the damn drafts. To Pam Simpson for her English teacher's confidence about commas and other editing expertise. Zenith Gross, all the food sections in this book are dedicated to you.

Mistakes herein are mine alone.

AN INDEPENDENT AUTHOR'S REQUEST

I hope that you enjoyed reading *Doppelgänger*. Please help support this independent writer by leaving a review on Amazon and Goodreads. Your comments are valuable and I would love to hear your feedback.

I am busily working on Book 4! Check my web page: www.susancory.com or my facebook page: www.facebook.com/authorsusancory for advance notification about the next books in the Iris Reid Series.

Conundrum and *Facade* are also available if you haven't caught up with Iris' earlier adventures.

Thank you!

Susan Cory